BEFORE THE FIRST

A KINGS OF HELL PREQUEL NOVELLA

By Alexis Maree

ALEXIS MAREE

CONTENT WARNING

This book contains scenes of dark natures which may trigger some readers - eg; torture, coarse language, scenes of sexual activity. Not all possible triggers have been mentioned.

By reading further, you, as the reader, are continuing with the understanding that this book has darker overtones and that not all possible triggers may have been mentioned. The author and any who contributed to this work cannot and will not be held accountable for a reader's state of mind or actions they may take due to the contents in this book

BEFORE THE BEGINNING
A KINGS OF HELL PREQUEL NOVELLA

OTHER BOOKS BY ME

<u>ALEXIS MAREE</u>

THE KINGS OF HELL SERIES:

The Kings of Hell — Cole
The Kings of Hell — Adrik
The Kings of Hell — Malik
The Kings of Hell — Harkyn
The Kings of Hell — Tamas

THE NEPHILIM SERIES:

Outcast

<u>T. MAREE</u>

THE LEAH REYNOLDS SERIES:

Sins in the Silence
Sins of a Daughter
Sins of the Past
Sins of the Enemy
Sins of the Forbidden
Sins of the Blood

STANDALONES

Falling for the Mountain Man
Colorful

<u>LUNA MAREE</u>

L'Amour Island
Her Sir & Sire
Theirs

BEFORE THE BEGINNING
A KINGS OF HELL PREQUEL NOVELLA

ALEXIS MAREE

DEDICATION

For you, my readers...

Thank you for loving my Kings and their mates as much as I do. Thank you so much for your kind comments and encouragement.
Your support has made this series possible.
Thank you.

xx

BEFORE THE BEGINNING
A KINGS OF HELL PREQUEL NOVELLA

ACKNOWLEDGEMENTS

Thank you as always to my family for your ongoing support and encouragement.

Thank you to Debra St James for your help and providing a second pair of eyes when I so desperately needed them.

Thank you, Adrianne Normanton, for fitting me into our crazily hectic schedule and providing much-needed feedback and advice.

As always, a huge thank you to my ARC team!

And last but never least, thank you to my readers. Your support and kind messages of encouragement and excitement push me to write, and I couldn't be more grateful for your love of my characters and the world they live in.

BEFORE THE BEGINNING
A KINGS OF HELL PREQUEL NOVELLA

READING ORDER

Mostly, the order is pretty straightforward, but with the Nephilim books now coming into play, things are a little different.
The reading order thus far is as follows to get the most out of the series:

The Kings of Hell – Cole

The Kings of Hell – Adrik

The Kings of Hell – Malik

The Kings of Hell – Harkyn

Outcast – The 1st Nephilim Book

The Kings of Hell – Tamas

Before The First – A Kings of Hell Prequel Novella

BEFORE THE BEGINNING
A KINGS OF HELL PREQUEL NOVELLA

CHAPTER ONE

DONOVAN

I closed my eyes and listened intently for the slightest hint of movement.

Their presence was cloaked from me, hidden, so that my other senses could not reach out and find them. I was alone, one against many, and despite not being able to see or sense them, I had the feeling that I was surrounded. This hunting trip had not gone as I had expected, and it had taken far too long already.

My eyes were peeled for any kind of movement, my ears straining for the merest whisper of sound.

The wind stirred gently through the tall canopy above, sending rays of light shimmering down upon the luscious grass and fallen leaves now littered on the forest floor.

Something moved.

I paused, my body strung tight as I closed my eyes to better find where the sound had come from, alerting me to a presence. My skin tingled with awareness, but I managed to slow my breath in order to concentrate more fully. There was *something...*

The air seemed thick with anticipation, as if the forest itself was holding its breath in preparation for the attack—

"Now!"

My eyes flew open at the battle cry shouted from somewhere above me. My head snapped up in time to see a body leap at me from the branches above and I had no time to move or brace before they were on me. I hit the ground with an *oomph* and was unable to push them off before another was on me, and another. I turned my head, looking for an escape and caught movement near a large tree. No, not *near* the tree… I frowned. It was as if a part of the tree had broken off from the large trunk and was walking toward me. The closer it got, the less it looked like a tree as the camouflage dissipated and I was left staring at a girl.

"Attack!" Another voice cried and I groaned as a body slammed into me from above once more.

"Restrain him!" someone shouted as I attempted to pull my hands up in front of me, preparing to defend myself. As if of its own accord, a vine whipped up from the ground and wrapped lightning-quick around my wrists.

"Hey!" I shouted, trying to push myself up, but the bodies kept me pinned.

"His ankles!"

"No, don't—" I tried, but I'd barely said the words before another vine erupted from the ground to bind my ankles.

"Kaela, his power!"

Oh, hell no. They weren't binding my power too! Gritting my teeth, I gathered my strength and forced away the ones holding me down and launched myself up, pulling on hellfire to burn away the vines binding me. The moment my limbs were free, I ran forward several steps, preparing to shadow out. I was outnumbered and limited.

I'd taken perhaps two steps when I was hit with an electric wave of power that stunned me for several precious seconds. While it was only seconds, it was all that was needed for the hoard of attackers to hit me again, this time from the back so that I landed hard on my front. I groaned as I hit the ground, and before I could think about my next actions, my hands were bound once more.

"I'll make you pay for this!" I shouted.

"How?" someone demanded, humor rich in their voice.

Oh, they thought they'd won, they thought this was the end. Well, they might have won this battle, but I would sure as hell make sure they lost the war.

Straining against my bonds was useless, and only seemed to make whatever was binding them tighten more. I snarled and someone snickered at my displeasure.

"Revenge *will* be mine," I warned, but the surrounding enemy simply laughed at my threat, obviously not believing my words, or worse… were simply not frightened by it. I could make them eat their words…

A new voice joined the group, this one older and filled with far more power. The earth beneath me seemed to ripple in awareness of their presence, a deep resounding heartbeat somewhere in the depths of the ground that seemed to reverberate in my body.

Her laughter was soft, musical, a soothing balm on searing wounds. Simply hearing it eased something inside me, cleansed me and made me ache to hear more of it.

"What have you girls done?"

With my face still pressed into the dirt, I tilted my head up to see a pair of bare feet come into my line of sight. I slowly raised my head to follow it up the long forest green skirt, to the leather belt cinched around her waist where several tools and a few knives hung, and up further to the pale pink blouse that had a couple of faded dirt stains. The curve of her breasts was prominent, and even locked down as I was, the feminine shape of her caused a physical reaction I tried quickly to repress.

Her hands were pressed to her hips, fingertips dirty as if she'd had her hands in the soil.

"We were practicing our magic, Mama," a small voice answered from my back.

The woman laughed softly again and sank to her knees beside me so I could take in her expression. I ignored the way my chest tightened and something deep inside me battled with itself. Her dee blue eyes were a startling midnight shade with woven strands of paler blue throughout. Her skin was sun kissed and smooth, her lips pouty and pale pink. Her raven black hair was pulled back in a braid, keeping it out of her face as she went about her day. The beauty of her always stunned me, but it was the woman within that never failed to leave me breathless.

"Did the girls play fair today, Donovan?" she asked.

I scowled in mock-anger. "They attacked en masse. I never even had a chance to defend myself."

Her eyes sparkled with humor and I felt a smile tease at my lips. "You were taken down by children, Demon King."

I raised my head as much as I could in the position I was in, projecting false indignation. "*Witch* children, Tabitha. They're Witches, and they do not play fair with their magic."

She let loose another laugh, and I felt my own smile grow, becoming entranced by the sound of it and the way she tipped her head back. I knew I was attracted to this woman—she knew it too, being a Witch and all—but I was a Demon King, and she had a family to consider. There would never be anything more than the friendship we'd cultivated between us, and as much as I sometimes wished there could be more, I was more than happy with what I had.

"Alright girls," Tabitha said when she regained her composure. "It is time to go get washed up, chores need to be done and dinner will be ready soon. Go check in with your parents first."

There was the sound of movement, equal mumbles of displeasure and agreement ringing out. The weight disappeared from my back as they moved away.

"Hey!" I shouted. "Someone, come back and untie me!"

Several of the girls giggled as they left me there, and I turned my head as a pair of small feet came back into view.

"It is not *really* tied up tight, Doni," Marlee told me with a very serious expression. I looked at the little girl and felt my heart melt at the sight of her baby face. It hadn't taken me all that long to get used to the nickname this little four-year-old had given me. No one else called me Doni, just her. She knelt closer to look at me as if she was concerned.

I broke free of my bonds and snatched her up before she could do more than widen her eyes and she giggled as I pulled her in tightly for a hug.

"Oh! I know, Miss Marlee. I was trying to trick you into coming closer so I could run away with you. And it worked!" I cried with an overzealous laugh.

"Silly, Doni. Mama would stop you," she pointed out.

I flicked a glance at her mother who sat watching us with affection and my smile softened. "I know, *Malishka*. Your mama would stop entire armies to get you back."

Marlee grinned and pressed each one of her little hands to my cheeks before pressing hard. I tried to talk, but the words came out unintelligible while she smooshed my cheeks. She giggled as I knew she would and released my face. I'd known this girl her whole life, and I'd started calling her *Malishka*—baby girl—from nearly the first moment I'd held her.

"Come on, Marlee. You have jobs to do, too," Tabitha reminded.

"Okay, Mama," Marlee agreed before she pressed a smacking kiss to my cheek. "Bye, Doni!"

She scrambled out of my arms before kissing her mother on the cheek as well and toddled off toward the cottage where they lived. I watched her go, that melting sensation in my chest burning bright and hot as I watched her. She was so little, but that girl—much like her mother—had me wrapped around her little finger.

"When did she get so big?" I mused aloud. I could remember the day I showed up to see how Tabitha was doing and she handed me this little bundle wrapped in a blanket. I'd never held a baby until that point, and almost immediately I'd been done for. I'd been entranced by her tiny features, her little cherub cheeks, that little mouth and impossibly small ears and fingers. She'd felt so fragile; I'd been afraid to so much as breathe in case I somehow hurt her.

Tabitha's husband had died six months prior, leaving her and her daughter without anyone to protect them. Not that they needed it with their magic, but the world was not a friendly place for

Witches and they had to give the impression of being normal humans.

"I know. She is growing up so fast."

A bittersweet expression passed over Tabitha's face, and I knew without her having to say it that she wished her husband had been alive to see it happen. If I could have brought him back for her, I would have. Despite the strange possessiveness I often felt when it came to her, I just needed to see her happy. Witnessing her pain and her tears was not an experience I ever wanted to have again. I already knew being with me was not an option for her— no matter the dreams and urges I sometimes had—and if her husband brought her that sense of love and light, then I wanted her to have it.

But some things could not be undone, and she understood that better than most.

"So, how did the girls really do?" she asked, bringing us back to the present situation.

I smiled and hitched my shoulder. "They're improving. Lena, with her camouflage, was incredible. I didn't know she was there until she moved. I couldn't sense any of them, not even Marlee. They're much faster than they used to be."

A year or so ago, a few of the Witches in the area had been set upon by Rogue Demons. Honestly, their numbers were so small that I never thought they'd go so far as to attack Witches, but apparently, they'd lost their minds along with their sense of loyalty when they pulled away from the armies of Hell. We'd get on top of them one day, but there were other things that felt more important at present.

In any case, they'd taken a Witch and her body had been discovered a week later. Since then, Tabitha had asked me to work with the children to help them learn to hide themselves from my kind and even improve their combat skills as their abilities grew. So, whenever I had time, I hunted the Witch children in the forest by their home and they improved a little every time. No, I wasn't using my full set of skills when I versed them, that would end up with them being hurt. But I wasn't lying when I said I couldn't sense them, and that was the biggest hurdle.

"Are they improving enough?" she asked.

I searched Tabitha's troubled face at her question, feeling the underlying sense of urgency there. "What's wrong?"

She sighed and looked away from me, using a random twig to draw patterns in the soil. "I do not know," she whispered softly and shook her head. "I just... I have this sense that something is coming, something big. I want to know what it is, what it means, but I lack the courage to fully reach out and touch it. Every time I think about it, I know I should prepare for whatever it is, but something inside me turns away from seeing it."

I swallowed hard at the tremor in her voice, and when she raised those beautiful blue eyes to meet mine, there was a sheen of tears there and a sliver of fear I'd never seen before.

The need to protect her rose swift and sharp, and I saw the way her breath caught when she felt my desperate need to act on my instinct. Her tears tore at me, the tremble of her lips making my stomach churn, and I had to push back the desire to fight back at this invisible threat.

"I won't let anyone hurt you. *Or* them," I whispered.

Her expression softened slightly and she slowly pushed herself up off the ground and brushed at her skirt to shake off the dirt and leaves. "You cannot make promises like that, Donovan. You have your realm to rule and responsibilities outside of us. I will not let you take on that kind of obligation, nor will I let myself rely on it."

I stood too and gently shackled her wrist with my fingers. The zap of electricity at our contact made my blood come alive with awareness and need, but her tears cut at me, and so I ignored how good it felt to touch her.

"You will not let yourself rely on me, but I insist that you do." Watery eyes met mine and I faced her more fully, refusing to let her look away. "Demand it of me, Tabitha. You could ask me for the moon and the stars and I would find a way to get them for you. There is nothing you could ask of me that I would not give my all to make happen. You and Marlee... you are important to me."

They were probably the *most* important thing to me. I don't know when it had happened or how, but from the moment I'd met this Witch, my world had begun to revolve around her.

"Donovan…"

"If there is something you're worried about, you need to tell me so I can be ready for it too. If you feel the girls need extra training, extra help, you need to tell me so I can give them all the help possible. I need to know what I'm up against so I can properly arm them and you against it."

"That's just it," she said and gently tugged her hand back. I let her go reluctantly, trying not to feel the ache of having her pull away from me. "I don't know what we are up against. Whenever I try to reach for it to get an understanding of what it is… it…" she trailed off, at a loss for words. "Something is preventing me from seeing it. All I know is that it is big, it is scary… and I am not sure if we will survive it."

Dread coiled low at her words. Witches were empaths, and some had that power to an extreme level where it was not only the emotions of others they could sense, but the mood of the day, the events that were yet to come. Some were so in tune they could feel the emotion of the earth beneath our feet and those who trod upon it.

If Tabitha said there was a Big Bad coming, then I believed her.

"Okay," I said softly and stepped in closer to her so she had to tip her head back to look at me. "Listen to me, Tabitha. Whatever this thing is that has you so frightened, I will be here with you to fight it. You and me. We'll do everything we can to fight it off, and we'll do it together."

"Donovan…"

"You're not asking this of me, Tabitha. I am offering. No, I am *demanding* you let me do this. Do you think I could stand it if anything happened to you? To Marlee? Do you think I could keep my head up around you if I let anything happen to the others you surround yourself with?"

She swallowed hard and I hoped she felt the intensity of my emotions. I needed her to understand this. If she was not willing to accept my feelings for her, that was fine. But she *would* understand my lack of tolerance for the thought of not doing everything in my power to protect her and Marlee.

"You have other responsibilities, Donovan. And I cannot afford to let myself rely on someone who might not be able to be there for us."

"I can only be there for you as much as you let me," I returned softly.

Her eyes burned up at me. I could see how she wanted to reach for me, how she wanted to lay her problems at my feet and lean on me for support, but she had learned the hard way to rely on herself. And where her daughter was concerned, there was no room for mistakes. Allowing someone else to do something for her she could not do herself was scary for her.

"You know me, Tabitha," I whispered, gently raising my hand to stroke her cheek. "What do you have to fear from letting me be there for you and letting me in?"

Her head tilted just the smallest amount, leaning into my touch. My breath caught at the merest sign of her softening toward me and her eyes remained locked with mine.

"You *know* what I would be risking."

Her words were soft, her reply short and to the point, but the layers to those seven words were far more. We weren't just talking about me helping her, about her letting me be there to protect them. Something burned hot and bright in my chest, a powerful ache that seemed to emanate from my very soul, and there was a demand inside me that I take action, that I somehow tie her to me this instant.

This was the first time she had ever acknowledged that there was something more between us than the friendship she'd offered me. She knew how I felt about her—despite what I told my brothers and anyone else who asked—but she'd masterfully managed to avoid talking about it in any shape or form in the past, and I'd respected her gentle boundaries and unspoken request not to push. I had been certain there were more feelings on her side for me, as well. But again, broaching the subject with her was like trying to capture a cornered animal. I feared if I pushed too hard, she'd run and I'd never catch her again.

Being in her life in any way was better than none at all.

"Is it really that much of a risk when you know how I feel about you?" I asked gently. A flash of something I could not decipher flickered in her eyes and she closed them with a small sigh. I was losing her, I knew I was. She was shutting down, building up her defenses to put that wall between us again. A part of me wanted to be mad at her for it, but I knew why.

"Donovan…"

I sighed and dropped my hand and she slowly raised her gaze to mine again, something like regret in her eyes. She didn't want to hurt me, I knew that.

Smiling softly so she could see I was okay, I shrugged. "Yeah… We've had this conversation before in some form or another."

"You know how much you mean to me," she whispered, a myriad of emotions in her eyes.

"I know," I agreed. "Maybe more than you would like."

Another beat of silence passed and she took a small step back. I didn't stop her this time, knowing I'd pushed things as much as I could for today. I wanted her in every way I could have her, in *any* way. If this was all I was going to get, then I'd find a way to be okay with it, but I'd never stop hoping for more.

"You'll keep practicing with the girls?" she asked, clearing her throat.

"Of course, and I'll make it a little more challenging from here on out."

She nodded and smiled gently, but it was for show. I'd spooked her, I'd pulled her out onto a ledge she'd tried desperately to avoid in the past and she needed some time to come to terms with it.

"Thank you, Donovan. I should… I should go," she said, backing up another step. I nodded and watched unblinkingly as she backed up another few steps before turning away from me.

"Tabitha?"

She turned back to me, wariness on her face. "Yes?"

I hesitated and let my breath out slowly. "I am here for you, always. All you have to do is call. No matter what else happens or doesn't happen, I am here. In every way that matters, you and Marlee are mine to protect. I will protect you and your family from whatever danger is coming with everything I have, with everything I am. There are no strings attached to that; I promise."

Those tears shimmered in her sapphire eyes again and her expression softened. "I know, Donovan. Thank you."

I watched her walk away, feeling her take yet another piece of me with her.

BEFORE THE BEGINNING
A KINGS OF HELL PREQUEL NOVELLA

CHAPTER TWO

TABITHA

"You allow that Demon King too close, Tabitha."

I bit back the sigh that wanted to escape as I pulled at the weeds in the garden. They were labeled as weeds, but if you were a Witch, you knew everything had a use. These would be used later on for a soothing tea to help the young one's sleep.

"Donovan is a friend," I reminded my twin sister, Bea, but I didn't stop what I was doing. In my family, the second pregnancy to any Witch would result in twin girls, and Beatrice and I were second born. We even shared the family mark on our arms, a birthmark in the shape of a star.

I could feel Bea's huff of frustration from where she stood at the garden gate, but I ignored it. It was a rule we tried to follow as a community. If one did not voice their feelings, we weren't supposed to point it out. There were exceptions, of course, but for the most part, we tried to allow everyone the chance to express themselves without telling them their feelings. Even so, Bea and I had always been closer than most, and I had to attribute it to being twins. No matter what, she always seemed to know what I was feeling, and I her. Which made hiding anything I felt for Donovan practically impossible. Thankfully, she allowed me the space to work through things on my own.

Usually.

"We are supposed to be neutral, Tabitha. We heal Angels and Demons, but we are not meant to choose sides. It is the way it has always been, and it should stay that way. Your friendship with the Demon King is clouding your objectivity."

I didn't want to talk about this, but some part of me knew she was right. We weren't supposed to befriend them, because getting to know them muddied the waters. How was I meant to heal an Archangel if I'd seen him run Donovan through with a sword at some earlier time? I winced at the visual in my head and banished it just as quickly.

"He is helping our girls to better their skills," I pointed out.

"And for the several years before he started training them? What was his purpose for hanging around then?" Bea pushed.

This time I let loose the sigh I'd bitten back before and dropped down on my knees to raise my face to the warm sun. The Summer Solstice was almost here, and we were all preparing for a feast and festival. The whole town got involved with decorations, celebrations, and music. There were feasts to be had all over, games, dancing, and people enjoying themselves. For regular humans, it was just about having fun. But for us Witches, it was a ritual and a time to give thanks to the Goddess Litha. Our rituals grounded us, and strengthened our bonds with the earth and each other.

"I know what you say is true," I finally muttered, bringing my gaze back to hers. "I know I should not be friendly with him; I know I should not allow him to be around us so often or to have any connection with our family."

"But?" she asked, knowing there was more.

That was the question, wasn't it? But *what*? Why *was* I letting Donovan be around? What was it about him that drew me in and held me hostage when my head told me it was not a good idea, but my heart and soul wept at the idea of letting him go? Why was he always on my mind? Why did I think of him whenever I needed someone to talk to? How did he seem to know when I needed someone and somehow show up?

The questions I had about the Demon King seemed nearly endless, and yet I never allowed myself to ask a single one. Why? Well... I was a coward, that was why. I was afraid of the answer. Whatever lay between me and Donovan felt powerful, too powerful to resist if I opened that door even a little. If I began poking at it, if I started asking questions and allowing space for it in my life, I knew it would take me over. I had more than just myself to consider now. I had Marlee, I had my twin sister, my cousins, aunts, uncles, and a community of Witches that—for whatever reason—seemed to look to me for guidance. That was to say nothing of the Witches I helped to hide from Demons and Angels alike.

A secret war was going on that none of us understood. Angels and Demons were taking Witches and keeping them for reasons we had no understanding of. My friendship with Donovan pre-dated our knowledge of these abductions, and he'd never given any indication that he meant to take any of us away. I'd never felt the smallest hint of deceit from him, and at the first sign, I would have taken my daughter and disappeared. Not only that, my family had all met him, and they kept tabs on him whenever he was around. His emotions and intentions were constantly being monitored by more than just me, and we all knew how he felt about us... about me. It was uncomfortable to have so many know a Demon King felt so strongly for me, but they could all see I was not giving in to whatever it was between us. It had been easier when Graham had been alive.

Thinking of my husband sent a sharp pain to my chest.

No, we hadn't been madly in love, but he had been my dearest friend growing up and he knew all about me being a Witch and was okay with it. We'd always been close, and so when it was suggested to us that we marry, it had felt natural. I felt great affection for him, and being with him had been easy. He was a good man; strong, steady, dependable. Never once did he press me for more than what I was willing to give. Neither of us were in love in the romantic sense, but we *had* loved each other. We'd been content, and that was more than many couples could say. He'd been protective of me, and he would have adored Marlee. It still hurt to know he'd never gotten the chance to hold her, to know her. He would have been an incredible father, and when I'd told him we were expecting a child, I'd never seen him so excited.

To know Marlee would never know her father, hurt.

I'd healed Donovan on two other occasions in the past, and both times he'd been grateful and even funny. I hadn't expected humor from him, and it had ignited our strange friendship. I'd almost been caught in the crossfire the second time I'd healed him and he'd protected me with his own body before dispatching the threat. He'd been determined to see me home safely after that, and from then on, he'd just been... there. He'd taken his time making up his mind about Graham. For whatever reason, he'd struggled to accept my then-fiancé, but when he saw how much Graham cared for me, he finally relented.

Graham had been wary of Donovan's presence at first, but soon came to like having him around, and the two had formed a distantly friendly bond. Neither were interested in hanging around with the other, but they were polite, which was more than I had expected.

"Tabitha?"

I jerked at the sound of my name and blinked at Bea who watched me with mild amusement.

"Sorry?"

She rolled her pale blue eyes. "We were talking. You were going to explain about the Demon King hanging around and why it was okay."

"Oh," I said and looked away, not sure what I was going to say to defend myself or his presence.

Bea sighed and leaned on the garden fence, her eyes seeing far more than I was comfortable with, but as my sister, I was used to this occurrence. I let my gaze drift over her deep auburn hair and the way the sun made it burn bright. We were twins, but we were not identical, and I sometimes found myself in awe of the deep red of her hair. "We all know, Tabitha. We see you together, we experience what you feel in his presence and what he feels for you. Our comfort is that his feelings are genuine, and not spawned from a need to possess you or your power. There's no manipulation or falseness."

"I won't let it happen," I whispered softly and forced myself to keep my eyes locked with hers. "I know it cannot happen, and I won't give in to it."

Her expression didn't give anything away, but I felt her doubt.

"What happened yesterday?"

I frowned. "Yesterday?"

"You sent the children inside to do their chores, and I watched the two of you from the kitchen window. He's never been shy about getting close to you, but you have always kept the space to maintain your boundaries. But yesterday... he touched you. I felt the shock of it from inside the house. I felt what his touch does to you, what it does to him. The boundaries you put in place shook to their foundations, and all he did was touch your cheek."

I swallowed hard and tried not to revisit the way I felt at his touch. I had never felt such a pull to anyone before, I didn't know such a feeling could exist. It was as if something in me recognized something in him, and the two were not meant to be separate. The yearning to meld those pieces together was stronger every time he came to see us. I knew the intelligent thing to do would be to tell him to leave and not come back. But the very thought of not seeing him again hurt me in a way I couldn't explain. It was soul-deep, and it dragged me into a dark place of desolation and mourning. How was that even possible?

"I think you need to reflect on your true feelings for the Demon King, Tabitha. Think long and hard, be true to yourself. But we are Witches of the earth. We cannot tie ourselves to something as dark as a Demon King. What we have allowed already feels too much, any more would be a catalyst for destruction, with repercussions of which we cannot yet see."

"I know," I whispered.

"I know you *know* it," she said, touching her temple. But her eyes were soft as she continued. "But you need to know it *here*," she said, touching the spot over her heart.

I didn't say anything to that, and she spared me a small, sympathetic smile before leaving me to my thoughts. The problem was... I *did* know it in my heart. And that's why it hurt so much to know I had to let him go.

~

"Higher!"

I couldn't help the grin on my face at hearing Marlee giggle. Her laugh was so contagious, and it lit up everything inside me to hear her happiness. When I rounded the corner of the cottage to see what she was doing, I paused mid-step as I watched Donovan toss her small body up into the air, the muscles in his biceps bulging with the action. My daughter's eyes were closed, her face serene and full of so much trust as the Demon below her held his arms out to catch her upon her descent.

Donovan's face was beaming with joy and... love. I knew he loved Marlee. He'd been in her life from the morning she was born, and he had never left. He adored her, he'd do anything for her... and damn it, that hurt so much. Because this just couldn't continue.

I'd made such a mess of things.

By allowing Donovan to be with us, I'd let him entrench himself in my daughter's life, and to tell him to leave now would hurt her. And why? Because I lacked the self-control to keep my feelings under control?

My heart nearly swelled out of my chest as I watched him nestle her against his heavily muscled chest and she wrapped her arms around his neck to press a loud smacking kiss to his stubbled cheek. God, I loved his facial hair and the way it accentuated the vision of masculinity he presented.

"Again, Doni?"

He grinned at the way she said his name and tapped the tip of her nose with his finger. "Maybe later, *Malishka*. Your mama wants to talk to me."

I startled at those words, but I shouldn't have been surprised that he knew I was there. Donovan turned to look at me, a devastatingly handsome smile on his face. Marlee followed his gaze and she beamed.

"Mama!"

My heart melted as she squirmed out of his embrace and came running over to me as fast as her little legs could carry her. I scooped her up and snuggled her close, breathing in the scent of her hair. "Hey, baby."

"Doni was throwing me *way* up in the air! I flew!" she squealed delightedly, her blue eyes so like mine shining brightly.

I grinned at her. "I saw!"

"She wanted me to go higher, but I was already terrified she would fly away on me," Donovan said as he joined us.

Marlee giggled. "Silly Doni, I can't *fly*."

He widened his eyes with mock surprise. "I don't know, I thought I saw you grow some wings for a moment."

I laughed lightly when Marlee looked excited at the idea.

"Marlee!"

We turned to see my sister calling for her, my niece and nephew at her side.

"We are going to the falls. Do you want to come?"

Marlee sucked in a breath so sharp I was worried she'd pass out from too much oxygen at once. Her wide eyes turned to me, a look of hope in her gaze. "Can I, Mama? Can I go?"

I brushed a kiss over her forehead. "Of course. Stay close to Aunty Bea, okay?"

Kissing my forehead, she wiggled out of my arms and threw her arms around Donovan's leg in a tight squeeze. "Bye, Doni!"

He leaned down to hug her, brushing a kiss over the top of her head. "Bye, *Malishka*. Have fun."

Without another second's hesitation, she ran off toward my sister with the sort of enthusiasm only a child can have. Bea looked from Donovan to me, the meaning of her look clear. I gave a tiny nod and watched as Bea took Marlee's hand and together, she and her children started away. I watched after them for a long moment, giving myself time to gather my strength and attempt to find the words that needed to be said.

"Tabitha."

I closed my eyes on Donovan's voice, hating the way it felt sliding over my skin as he said my name. Why did this Demon King affect me in ways no other ever had? It shouldn't be possible to feel such a way toward him. I knew what he did, what he was capable of. The destruction and violence alone went against everything I was and everything I strived to achieve.

And yet...

"I can't—"

"Don't," he interrupted sharply.

My eyes snapped upward and I found him standing much closer than he was before, his expression near tortured. He shook his head, his chest rising and falling sharply as if he was struggling to remain calm. "Do not do this. I know what you are going to say, and I am begging you... do not say it."

"I must," I returned sadly. "If you know, then you understand why."

"But I do not agree," he shot back. "Why does this have to end? I would die before I let anyone touch you or your family—"

"But we are not your responsibility, and I cannot let my judgement cloud because of how I feel about you."

Donovan hesitated, his eyes desperate, but something about my words struck him temporarily silent. "Tell me."

"Tell you?"

"Tell me how you feel about me, Tabitha."

My heart slammed hard in my chest at his request and I took a retreating step backward, shaking my head.

"I cannot."

"You can. Tell me."

"Donovan—"

"Have I ever asked you to stop doing what you do? Have I ever been displeased with you for healing my enemy? Have I ever threatened you or let you down after you healed someone who has previously done me or mine wrong?"

I shook my head, my eyes stinging with tears. "No."

"Then why does this have to end? I would never stop you from doing what you are supposed to do."

"But *I* would!" I shouted, pressing my hands to his chest to stop him advancing on me. "*I* would stop healing them. *I* would become angry with them, become biased. I cannot afford to let myself hate them and hesitate when they need help, or it could cost them their life, and I will carry that guilt until the day I die. It would eat me up, and I do not want to risk such an existence."

"You wouldn't," he protested.

I shook my head and steadied my breathing before replying. "I would."

Donovan's gaze darted over my face, questions and emotions flowing across his expression.

"I would stop, Donovan. For you, for what they do to you—if I let myself think about you like that, think about—about us… How could I stand to heal the very beings who try to kill you on a daily basis?"

He looked torn, his expression part devastated, part hopeful. He reached for me, sliding his hands up to grip my forearms. I stopped backing away, and my arms weakened as he stepped closer with my hands on his chest.

"This… what we have? Whatever this is between us… it is not normal, Tabitha. It is powerful and unique, and it feels too precious to ignore."

"Exactly," I agreed glumly. "It is *not* normal. My family have already noticed how things are between us, and they have voiced their concerns. I cannot allow for this to happen, Donovan. I just… please don't make this harder than it already is."

His chest continued to rise and fall as he struggled for control, and I closed my eyes on the wrenching sensation in his chest that mirrored the one in mine. Why was this so hard? Why did saying goodbye to a Demon King cause me so much pain?

"Tab—"

With a sob wrenching from somewhere deep in my soul, I pulled back out of his embrace and staggered back several feet. I glanced up at him through tear-filled eyes and shook my head. I didn't need to clearly see the features of his face to know the hurt I was causing him; I could feel every iota of it.

"I am sorry, Donovan. Maybe..." I trailed off, words failing me. Because deep down, I knew there was no *maybe,* there was no chance for us, not in this life, and probably never in another.

Without another word, I spun on my heel and fled for the cottage.

And he let me go.

ALEXIS MAREE

CHAPTER THREE

DONOVAN

For thousands of years, I had swept through the ages, torturing and maiming, doing my level best to create soldiers for the legions of Hell. I punished the wicked and took pleasure in making sure they met their fate without any hesitation or remorse.

I knew pain, it was my whole reason for existing.

And yet, try as I might, I struggled to find a way to ease my own. It had been two months, and the only time I laid eyes on her was from afar. Tabitha had kept to her decision and refused to interact with me, even in the smallest sense. I still went by the cottage to see the other Witches, to train the young ones and make sure they were prepared for whatever foreshadowing of doom Tabitha was afraid of. But she made sure never to come out and see us. If ever a message needed to be conveyed, it was her twin sister, Bea, who passed it along.

Even though Tabitha refused to see me, she didn't stop me from seeing Marlee, and I was grateful to her for that. Marlee wasn't mine, I knew that, but I'd been in her life since her first day, and I loved her more than I knew I could love someone. She wasn't mine, but she *felt* like mine.

I did my best to put on a brave face for my little *Malishka*, but she was a Witch to her core, and she could feel that all was not right with me. The other girls, too, knew something was up, but judging by the exchanged looks between some of the older ones, they'd been clued in to what the issue was.

I flinched suddenly when a sharp pain zapped up my arm and I raised my head to glower at my brother.

"What?"

Cole grinned. "Fuck, who pissed in your whiskey?"

I grunted a response but didn't bother to reply more than that.

"Seriously, Donovan. You've been a miserable asshole for weeks now, what gives?" Tamas asked before downing the rest of his drink. I glared at my other brother and let my eyes skate around the dimly lit tavern we were in. Humans mulled around in groups, some singing and joking, others just talking or sitting quietly. It was a good spot to go to when we didn't want to be interrupted but still wanted to be on Earth.

"Nothing."

Tamas made a sound of disbelief and Cole shook his head with a small smirk. Sure, I was miserable, but that wouldn't stop my brothers from poking at me until I snapped. That was part of the fun for them, not that I wouldn't have done the same if the roles were reversed.

There was a small ripple in the air before Corvin took a seat beside me. I glanced at him and he grinned.

"What's with the sour face?"

I rolled my eyes. This fucker loved nothing more than to give us shit when we were down, grinning and poking until we either snapped out of it, or just plain *snapped*.

"He won't tell us," Cole answered for me.

"Obviously it has something to do with Tabitha," Devlin said as he appeared on my other side and took a seat.

"Well, we figured that much. But what happened exactly? Did she break up with you?" Tamas asked. I inwardly sighed as Corvin ordered a round of drinks, and I frowned at the number he called for.

"Nine?" I asked.

"Yeah, the others are on their way," Corvin answered with a shrug. This time I sighed aloud and closed my eyes as an ache started at the base of my neck. Alright, so I'd been a bit of a bastard since Tabitha had put space between us, but I was in no mood for whatever kind of fucked up intervention this was turning into.

"So?" Tamas prompted, bringing me back to his question.

"No, she didn't break up with me because we were never together," I answered stiffly.

"Not for lack of wanting… on your end, at least," Cassius pointed out as he too, joined the table.

"We were never together because we're friends," I rebutted, but the words tasted like ash on my tongue.

There was a snort from further down the table and I raised my gaze enough to meet Malik's amused stare from where he stood. "Friends my ass. You're head over heels for the Witch, and it's kinda pitiful watching you tag after her like a lovesick puppy."

I was up and at his side before I had time to think, my fist colliding with his chin. His head snapped back, but he was on me a second later. The pain of his punch was a welcome distraction from my constant state of misery and before I knew it, we were in an all-out brawl on the tavern floor.

There was a sudden shifting sensation, and I was yanked away from Malik, a strong forearm around my neck to hold me in place.

"Enough!" Adrik shouted, and it was only then that I realized we were outside in a quiet meadow, the final rays of the sun casting brilliant colors across the velvet sky. One of them had to have shadowed us away from the humans.

"Get your fucking hands off me," I snarled, and the arm holding me back disappeared. Corvin gave me a curious look as I staggered away from him and I glanced around to see all my brothers looking at me with a mix of amusement and confusion. "Seriously, what the fuck is wrong with you? Out with it,"

Harkyn demanded, crossing his arms over his massive chest.

I shook my head and dragged in a steady breath. Normally, I never lost my cool like that, but I was angry and was helpless to change anything.

"It's not anything, really. Things are just… complicated."

"Be a little more vague, brother. Some of us might get the slightest clue as to what the fuck you're on about," Devlin snarked sarcastically.

"Did you make a move on your girl only to have her reject you?" Malik asked. I glared and he grinned despite the blood on his lips.

"No."

"Is she marrying someone else?" Adrik guessed.

"No."

"Did she ask you to leave her alone?" Cassius tried next.

I hesitated in answering before I shook my head. "No."

"You hesitated," Corvin pointed out. "We're getting warmer."

"For fuck's sake," I hissed. "It's nothing like that. Look, she is a Witch, I am a Demon King. We shouldn't even be friends!"

"Yeah, so? All of us have been telling you that for years. What's changed?" Harkyn asked.

I scrubbed my hands over my face roughly before dropping them to my sides. "Tabitha has realized how complicated our loyalties can make things… for her. She's worried about staying impartial and what it would mean if she can't. She doesn't want the death of any being on her hands because she hesitated in healing them due to her friendship with me."

"So… what? You're not going to see her anymore? I thought you were helping with the Witch children?" Cole pointed out.

"I'm still working with the kids," I answered, an image of Marlee bursting across my mind and causing my chest to constrict. With everything my brothers knew about Tabitha and our friendship, they didn't know about Marlee. For some reason, it felt important to me to keep her existence quiet. It was another way to protect her since we couldn't always count on our Demons to stay loyal. The Rogue Demons were proof enough of that. If my brothers ever slipped up and spoke about Marlee in front of any of them, word would spread that she existed and that I had a weakness. I'd die before painting that target on her back.

"So… you just won't see *her*?" Harkyn guessed.

I shrugged. "Pretty much."

"That fucking sucks," Corvin answered after a small silence, his hand coming to rest on my shoulder where he squeezed it once in commiseration. "I'm sorry, brother."

"It is what it is. I'm not going to force her to be around me if she doesn't want to be," I replied morosely.

"And this is the reason you've been such a miserable asshole these last few weeks?" Cassius prodded.

Tipping my head back to growl at the night sky, I turned away from them and tried to find patience.

"Yeah, sure," I answered and turned toward them again. "If you don't mind, I need to be anywhere but here."

There were a few mumbled insults I brushed off, but before I could shadow away, Devlin called me back. "We're here, Donovan. If you need us, just call."

~

"Great work, all of you. I am seeing a lot of improvement. Head on home, and we will continue this lesson next time," I called out to the children who had been improving greatly in the last few lessons. Several girls waved or called their thanks before they headed in the direction of their homes.

It had been several days since my *intervention* with my brothers, and I was no better than I was before it. I was still lost on what to do.

"Thank you, Donovan," Khalani said, smiling. I nodded to the young woman who was maybe fourteen. She and the other older girls had taken a more serious approach to their training lately. I wasn't sure if they too felt the sense of foreboding Tabitha had, or if they had been told to learn all they could from me for another reason. Either way, it was in the older girls I'd seen the greatest improvement.

I staggered slightly as something slammed into my leg, and I looked down to see Marlee wrapping herself around me, her bright blue eyes shining up at me, her long black hair tied back so it stayed off her face.

"Doni!"

My heart melted at her voice, at the way she looked at me, and I felt a sincere grin break over my face as I leaned down to pick her up.

"Hey there, *Malishka*. You did *so* good today," I praised.

"You did really hard lessons today, Doni," she pointed out with a pout.

I tapped the tip of her nose and smiled. "Yes, but I only do hard lessons so you get better at handling your power. I want you to be as safe as possible. And you are doing much better."

Her smile was genuine, but it slowly slid from her face to be replaced by a look of sadness.

"What's wrong, Marlee?"

She sighed, her wide eyes filled with concern. "Mama is sad. It feels the same as in here," she said, pressing a hand to my chest. My heart clenched painfully at her words. Marlee gasped and I did my best to pull a mental shield up between us so she wouldn't feel it.

"Why are you so hurt?" she asked, her blue eyes shiny with unshed tears. "Did someone hurt you?"

I opened my mouth to answer, but words temporarily failed me. Someone *had* hurt me, but I'd walked into the situation knowing on some level that pain was the only outcome. And yet it hadn't stopped me from coming back every day, eager and willing to put myself in a position to become wounded.

"It is a little complicated, Marlee," I finally answered.

She pouted and a spark of amusement lit within me at her expression. She was so fucking adorable, and sometimes she looked so much like her mother.

"I want you to stay here more... like you used to. But Mama says you can't, but she will not tell me why. Why can't you stay, Doni? You used to be here *all* the time. I haven't seen you properly in *ages*," she complained, and my already constricted heart twisted at knowing she was missing me.

"I know, *Malishka*, I know. And I am so sorry. There are things that make it hard for me to be here as often as I'd like, and I am not sure if they will ever change. But I will *always* come for you if you need me," I tried to soothe, holding her closer as she continued to play with the collar of my shirt.

"Mama asked you not to come back, didn't she?" Marlee whispered without looking at me.

I hesitated. "What makes you think that?"

She shrugged, but I waited. Finally, she sighed and answered, her tone miserable.

"I heard Aunt Bea telling Colleen that Mama had spoken to you, and it meant you will not be around as much. Why did Mama ask you to go away? I love you, Doni, and Mama does too."

Fuck, that hurt. This girl…

Sighing, I slowly lowered us to the ground and held her close to me as I closed my eyes and tried to focus on soaking in every moment of hugging my girl again.

"I am not even going to tell you that eavesdropping is rude, you know it is," I began, watching her little face screw up in a frown. I bit back a smile and felt the urge disappear altogether when I tried to phrase what had to be said in a way that would make sense to her.

"Marlee… Do you know what I am?"

She tipped her head to the side in confusion. "You're my Doni."

I smiled. "Yes, I am. And you are my *Malishka*… but you're also a Witch. Do you know what *I* am?"

Her face shone with innocence and curiosity, and I had my answer.

"My kind… we are not known for being good. A lot of people see me or others like me, and they think we will hurt them, and that we will hurt the people they care about."

"You won't!" Marlee cried defensively.

"No, I won't," I assured. "But I *am* very powerful, and that makes some people scared. Do you know what Witches are meant to do? Like you and your mama?"

She thought about this and shrugged. "We do spells and we heal."

I smiled. "Yes. Your mama, other Witches... you are all born with special gifts that make it possible to heal Angels *and* Demons. All Witches are meant to heal *all* beings. You are not supposed to choose only one kind to heal."

She frowned but nodded in understanding, waiting for me to continue.

"Well, you see, the problem is that I get into fights with Angels sometimes. They do *not* like me, and I have a lot of reasons not to like them."

Her eyes went wide, and I monitored Marlee carefully to see if she was scared of me, but all I felt was surprise and an eagerness to know more.

"I met your mama one day when she healed me after I had been hurt by an Angel. After she was done healing me, she left to heal an Angel, one of the ones who had hurt me," I continued.

Her eyes went wide in disbelief. "But why? The Angel *hurt* you."

"Yes, he did. But you, as a Witch, are not meant to choose who you heal. If someone is in pain, your job is to heal them."

She seemed to understand and so I continued. "This is the problem we're facing, *Malishka*. You and your mama, you mean everything to me. I would do *anything* for the two of you. And your mother... She cares for me too, a lot more than she wants to admit. But if she keeps staying around me, and I get hurt again, she isn't going to want to heal the Angel who hurt me. And that is not what Witches are meant to do. You are not supposed to *choose* who to heal, you are just supposed to do it, to keep the peace."

"But I don't want to heal an Angel if they hurt you," she lamented.

I squeezed her tighter. "I know, *Malishka*. But if you didn't, you would feel bad if the Angel died when you could have saved it, and I won't let you feel guilty for that," I explained, feeling the smallest part of me ease when I realized that was true. Marlee loved me, she cared for me, and her world was being shaped by what we allowed to happen here and now. If she stayed this attached to me, she would never be the Witch she was meant to be. The part of me that had just healed suddenly died when I realized what I had to do.

Tabitha had been right.

Of course she had been. On some level, I'd understood her reasons for putting space between us, but I hadn't liked it. Hearing how biased Marlee was toward me already just drove the point home.

I had to stay away. It was the only way she would be able to properly fulfil her duty as a Witch and not face repercussions. I'd heard of Witches misusing their power or denying their purpose, and it resulted in a backlash that usually ended with them losing their magic. I couldn't allow her love for me to cause this to happen to her.

I refused to be the catalyst for something so abhorrent.

"But why do you have to stay away now?" Marlee asked softly, her little voice breaking my heart. I steeled myself so I wouldn't cry or run away with her, and instead drew in a slow, steadying breath.

"I am staying away to make it easier for your mother, for you. It's safer this way. There are people who want to hurt me, and if they know how much I care for the two of you, they might try to hurt you to hurt me."

Marlee buried her face against my neck, her small arms wrapping tightly around me, and I bowed my head over hers as I closed my eyes. I loved this little girl. I hated letting her go, but it was for the best. Maybe it would be better still to introduce them to Adrik or one of the others and have their sessions taken over by them. This was too painful.

"We should get you back inside now. Your mama will be looking for you," I whispered with a rasp in my voice.

She didn't say anything to that, she just squeezed me tighter.

Carefully, I got to my feet with her in my arms and started toward the cottages. I'd have to talk to Tabitha about one of my brothers coming in my stead and allow her and the other Witches to get a read on them. I knew my brothers wouldn't wish anyone here any harm, they were good, despite what lies were told about us.

The front door to the cottage opened as I approached and Bea appeared in the doorway, her concerned gaze on Marlee.

"Is she okay?"

I cleared my throat. "She's fine."

Her expression cleared to one of understanding and she nodded slowly. I came to a stop and gently rubbed Marlee's back.

"*Malishka*, it's time for you to go inside."

"No." Her voice was muffled against my neck, and I felt a dampness from her tears on my skin.

I sighed, my heart wrenching. "Marlee, you have chores to do, you have to let me go to do them."

"If I let you go, you are never going to come back."

I closed my eyes on the blade in my heart and forced myself to keep my shield up to protect her. I took an extra second to make sure there was no sadness in my voice when I answered. "Never say never, *Malishka*."

She pulled back to look at me, thick lashes spiky with tears. Her cheeks were pink with her rise of emotions, and her eyes were wet. "I want you to come back, Doni."

I forced a smile. "I will. If it's not tomorrow or the next day, I'll come back eventually. I could never leave you forever. I will always need to make sure you're okay. And hey," I said softly and knelt on the ground as I placed her on her feet. I brushed at the tears on her cheeks and forced myself not to sound like my heart was being shredded.

"You're a Witch, Marlee. You have special senses. You can sense me before you see me, right?"

She nodded and swiped at her nose with the back of her hand.

I smiled. "So, even if you don't see me, there will be times where you can sense me. Just know in those moments, I'm checking in on you. I am making sure that you and your mama, and all the other Witches here are safe. Even if you can't see me, you will feel me."

"But I *want* to see you!"

"Marlee—" Bea started.

"No!" she cried and stomped her feet. "I don't want you to go."

"And I'll never be gone, not really," I tried to soothe.

A sob broke free of her lips and tears began to trek down her soft cheeks. Fuck, could anything hurt worse than this? Steeling myself, I drew in another breath, feeling as though I was drowning in her misery.

Marlee threw herself at me again and I didn't hesitate to hug her back.

"I love you, Doni," she cried.

I closed my burning eyes and hugged her tighter. A Demon King I may be, but I'd never been subjected to this kind of pain before.

"I love you too, *Malishka*. I always will."

I held her for several long moments before I had to unhook her arms from around my neck. For a moment I thought she might protest, that she might make it harder than it already was, but she hesitated when looking at my face. Her small hand came up to touch my cheek and I watched her try desperately to stop crying. Young she might be, but she was a Witch, fully aware of my pain even if she didn't feel the full force of it.

"You be good for your mama, okay?"

She nodded as Bea placed a hand on her shoulder and I stood, slowly backing away.

It was an effort to drag my eyes from her face, but when I did, I caught Bea's sympathetic gaze and she nodded at me once. It was for the best, I knew it was.

But *fuck* it hurt.

BEFORE THE BEGINNING
A KINGS OF HELL PREQUEL NOVELLA

CHAPTER FOUR

TABITHA

I was drawn to the cottage and the pain radiating from there. It was real pain, but it wasn't physical. I dropped the basket with clothes by the back door and was about to go inside to see what the problem was when a figure stormed past the cottage. Donovan's stiff form strode away, his shoulders rigid and fists clenched. There was practically a cape of vulnerability and pain flowing from behind him, and I was helpless to ignore it

"Donovan," I called before I could stop myself. I hurried after him, reaching him as he rounded another corner. The second my hand brushed his forearm, he spun on the spot and gripped my arm, simultaneously pushing me against the stone wall of the building behind me.

"Don—"

"I'm leaving," he ground out, his eyes filled with so much anguish it caused a ripple of pain within me.

"Leaving?" I asked, dumbfounded. "But... the girls. What about Marlee?"

He ground his teeth and I watched as he released a breath through clenched teeth. "It is because of Marlee that I'm leaving. She is too attached. Her actions and feelings are being warped by my presence here, and I won't be the reason her magic backfires or dies out on her."

"But…"

He shook his head and closed his eyes. I felt his tenuous hold on his control, the way he tried desperately to call forth the calm he usually held.

"And their lessons?" I whispered, constantly aware of that niggling sense of doom in the back of my head and the fact that it was getting more intense.

Donovan took several long moments to reply. "I will ask my brothers if they are up for the task, and then we'll reach out for you and whoever else you need to meet them. They will continue the lessons. I can't do it, Tabitha. It's too hard, it hurts too much and Marlee—" his voice cut out, his tone pained and expression near ravaged as he said my daughter's name.

I knew he loved her; he had always loved her. He was the nearest thing she had to a father, and I knew he wanted to do everything in his power to protect her as a father should.

"Did you say goodbye?" I asked in a whisper.

He nodded, forcing another breath of air out before dragging in another. "Yes. She is upset. She needs you."

"And you?"

"What about me?" he asked, frowning.

"Who do you have? I feel your pain, too. Who do you have to go back to?"

He shook his head. "I am a Demon King, Tabitha. Pain is my forte. I am far older than you can fathom, and I can handle my own emotional wounds."

Even as he said it, I knew he was banking on his thousands of years of practice more than his actual knowledge of how to handle something so personally painful. His blue eyes I'd always found so entrancing were dark with pain and regret. He didn't know how to cope with this any more than I did.

"Will you be okay?" I asked, my voice cracking. I hated this, hated myself. I didn't want him to leave, and I wished this wasn't necessary. But I had sowed the seeds of our demise a long time ago, and now it was time to pay the price.

Donovan didn't bother to respond, we both knew the answer. His dark eyes scanned my face, and through all the pain I felt the stirrings of desire, of need. My breath caught as the feeling grew within him, so hot and bright that it caught fire inside me.

"Tabitha…" he trailed off, and it felt like there was a warning in his voice, a chance for me to leave before he let go of his control and took what he wanted, what we both wanted.

"Are you still leaving?" I murmured, my gaze darting to his lips.

"I have to."

I hesitated. "No matter what?"

He swallowed hard, and I dragged my gaze up his face to see the indecision in his eyes before the painful truth set in. "Yes."

"Then kiss me," I whispered, tugging him closer.

He didn't need me to say anything more. The space between us closed in an instant, and his mouth slanted over mine. I gasped at what felt like sparks on my tongue as his touched mine, and I swallowed the rumbling moan he let loose. Finally doing the one thing we'd both been desperate to do felt like nothing else.

It was... electric. It was heated and intense, and like something raw inside me was finally soothed. Donovan's hands slid around my waist to haul me against his hard frame, and he backed me up so that I was pressed tighter against the stone wall.

It gave the phrase *between a rock and a hard place* an entirely new meaning.

I wrapped my arms around him. Feeling him against me after years of keeping our distance was euphoric. Everywhere his skin touched mine felt like fire licking up my body, burning hot and bright, urging us to go up in an inferno of flames together.

"Moya lyubov'" he murmured. The Russian endearment made my heart clench. *My love.* Hearing him say it, even in another language, made everything so much harder. His hands dropped to my waist as he rocked his hips against mine, and a startled moan escaped me.

I *felt* his desire build, grow, turn into something almost feral with need. I was being washed along in the rapids of our desire, too far gone to try and come up for air.

Mine. Mine. Mine.

The words were there in my head, urging me to mark him in some way, to claim him in a way that would make it impossible to take back. He was mine and I was his. Nothing in the world seemed clearer than that.

His mouth left mine to skate down my neck as he lifted me. I wrapped my legs around his waist, rocking against him, desperate for more, oblivious to anything else but the man in my embrace. His lips, teeth, and tongue were driving me to the point of insanity, and I *needed* him.

"Donovan," I panted, my body overheated and mind a muddled mess. Nothing made sense anymore. There was no up or down, there was no right or wrong, and there was certainly no good and bad. There was just us, just this. Somehow, we were one in the same and we had been apart far too long.

"Tabitha." My name whispered in a desperate moan caused muscles to spasm with need between my legs. I needed him in more ways than I knew how to explain.

His hands were everywhere, just like mine. I couldn't stop touching him, tasting him. He was devouring me, hungry for more, and I was more than willing to let him take me over because I knew I was doing the same for him.

"Don—"

"Tabitha!"

My name was shouted from somewhere inside the house, and it was like ice water on the inferno raging between us. We paused, our lips parted by the merest millimeter, our breaths intermingling as we took a moment to realize how carried away we had gotten.

Donovan's deep blue eyes stared down into mine, a few seconds of confusion as the haze between us lifted, and then a tidal wave of despair and longing.

This was it.

We were done.

Neither of us moved for the longest time. Our eyes remained locked as we took our time coming to terms with the harsh realities we faced. I didn't understand how this was possible. How could I feel something so intense and powerful with this Demon King? Why did it feel as though I was cutting myself in half by letting him go and leaving me with only half of my faculties?

Why did it feel like my soul was splintering?

I opened my mouth to speak, but no words came out. There were no words to speak at this time. We both knew what had to be done. We both knew what our positions were and what was necessary. What we wanted didn't matter, it couldn't matter.

Whatever lay between us was scarily powerful and all-consuming, but it put others at risk, it put my family at risk, and his.

There was no way this could work.

Slowly, Donovan let me slide down the length of his body, and with every inch that brought my feet closer to the ground, I felt like I was losing a piece of myself. The moment my feet were under me, my knees began to shake, but I locked them, refusing to fall under the weight of what had to be done.

Not once did he take his eyes from mine.

I hoped he knew I felt his pain, and that it was matched by my own. I hoped he knew this wasn't an easy decision for me, and that staying away these last few weeks had almost killed me. I hoped he knew that hearing my daughter giggle in his arms had stabbed at me every day, knowing it would all come to an end.

I hoped he knew.

Slowly, Donovan leaned back in to kiss me, but this wasn't like before. There was no desperation, no all-out heat and passion. It was painful and slow. It was powerful and filled with so much emotion.

It was goodbye.

My lips clung to his as he pulled away, and when I opened my eyes to see him again. Torment and anguish reflected back at me. He didn't say anything, and neither did I. There was nothing more to say.

With one last look, Donovan stepped away from me, and with a whip of wind, he was gone.

CHAPTER FIVE
DONOVAN

The days after leaving were some of the worst I'd ever endured. The memory of Marlee's pleading sobs woke me from sleep, her sweet face and wet cheeks tearing at me, piling on the guilt and despair.

But it was Tabitha's clinging lips and warm body that left me in a state of pain and need that no one but her could ease. The taste of her kiss still lingered on my tongue; the feel of her soft curves wrapped in my arms felt somehow ingrained on my brain. There was no forgetting her now, no pushing her to the back of my mind until the day came that she would fade from my memory. No, Tabitha was in my system now, in my blood, and it was a torment of my own making.

My brothers knew why my mood was so foul and had done their best to give me space. Cassius was going to meet with Bea and some of the Elder Witches for them to approve him to continue teaching the young ones. He had volunteered, and I'd been grateful. While it killed me not to be there, it was for the best.

I didn't think I'd have the ability to walk away a second time.

It shamed me to admit that I'd only had the strength to check up on them once, and even then, I'd barely forced myself to turn away. Marlee and Tabitha had both been in their garden working. Tabitha felt my presence first, but other than a slight stiffening of her body, she didn't give away that she knew. Marlee noticed moments later, and she hadn't been as quiet. She'd gasped and shot to her feet; eager eyes swinging around to try and catch a glimpse of me. My heart swelled and shattered at the same time, and the sound of her small voice calling my name damn near destroyed me.

Turning away from them took a feat of strength I was unprepared for.

It was only days since I'd last talked to them or held them, but it felt like eons. Something inside me ached to be around them, to simply soak in their presence and bask in their warmth. I was on the outside looking in, watching over something I could never have again. There was no real way to explain it, but it felt like they were *meant* to be mine. Being away from them felt unnatural.

Another few days slid by, slow and creeping. I was back watching them, unable to stay away for very long. Tabitha was playing with the girls in the garden. The other Witches were out with them, playing, doing their chores, but each and every one of them was on guard, their eyes shifting in the shadows and the trees to keep an eye on me. Perhaps they worried I'd snatch my girls away.

They had reason to worry.

I had never felt so out of my depth in my entire existence, never felt so bereft or alone. Every hour was torture, and it puzzled me to no end. I'd made friends with humans before, Witches too. I'd suffered the knowledge that I'd lose them one day, either due to a change in circumstance or death. Losing people was nothing new to me.

But I'd never felt as though any of them were a *part* of me. I'd fallen in love with Tabitha, I was honest enough with myself to admit it, and I knew she was in love with me, no matter how hard she fought it. Marlee was my girl, she was my daughter in every way that counted, and being separated from her *killed* me. Yet, this was about more than love.

While I couldn't say for sure that I'd ever really fallen in love before, I knew the pain I was in was due to more than just being separated from the woman and child I saw as my own. Something else was at play here, something powerful and... and new. I couldn't explain it.

After too many drinks one night, I'd attempted to explain this feeling to Cole, but he didn't seem to grasp it, or maybe he couldn't. As far as I could tell, none of my brothers had ever felt anything as powerful as this before, or if they had, they were being stubbornly tight-lipped about it.

I was certain they hadn't, however. To leave me alone in my misery without answers or someone else who could relate was a cruelty we would not bestow on one another.

Marlee's giggle drew me back to the present, and my heart swelled, even as my soul wept. I felt like I had lost them, as if they were dead and forever out of my reach. But they weren't. They were right *there*.

Somehow, this was worse. I knew logically that it wasn't. Seeing them alive and capable of joy was a gift, I *knew* it, but I couldn't feel it yet through my own grief. Fuck, I was an asshole. Why couldn't I just be happy that they were alive and well? Why couldn't I find solace in knowing that they would continue on in this life, thriving and growing, even if I couldn't be a part of it. Their safety was being seen to by my brother—or would be, once the lessons started. I could still check in on them to make sure they were okay. Why couldn't I shake this feeling?

My breath caught painfully when Tabitha's eyes met mine. I was too deep in the forest to actually be seen by the human eye, but Tabitha knew me so well. She could find me in the darkest pits of Hell with her eyes closed.

The same sense of loss and grief was there in her eyes, in her soul. Regret and sorrow for being the cause of my pain was there too. I didn't want her to experience remorse at my sadness. I wanted her to be happy, even if it was without me.

But this was our reality now.

Before I acted rashly, I tore my gaze from hers. Closing my eyes and letting the shadows envelope me and take me back to my realm. Back to my lonely realm haunted by memories of the life I'd had and lost.

~

TABITHA

I couldn't say I hadn't seen this coming.

I'd known from the very start that becoming involved with the Demon King, in any capacity outside of healing him, would result in nothing but pain and loss. I'd known it, and yet I had been unable—or perhaps unwilling—to disentangle myself from him. Donovan was... mine.

I became frustrated with myself every time I used that word to describe him to myself, but nothing else fit quite as well. Somewhere to the depths of my soul, I knew he was mine. I knew I was his, and that this separation was unnatural.

I huffed and used the small trowel to dig deeper into the ground. No, what was *unnatural* was the bond I'd created for him. The warped sense of right and wrong I'd instilled in my own daughter was the real issue. I was a Witch, for Aradia's sake! Me and mine were meant to heal and protect, we were meant to cultivate the earth and spread peace. The unnaturalness was my insane feelings for Donovan.

My breath hitched on a broken sob and I threw the trowel and closed my eyes.

Everything about our bond was abnormal. I *knew* it in my head. From a young age I'd been taught the importance of neutrality, and until the Demon King, I'd had no trouble at all in abiding by that rule.

Unnatural. I was repeating the word to myself over and over, hoping to remind my heart and soul of what he was and what he was created to do. I was trying to remind myself that Witches and Demons did *not* become attached to one another because that way led to disaster. And yet…

With the exception of my daughter, nothing had felt more natural to me than spending time with Donovan. The two of us together felt *right*. I couldn't explain it, nothing about it made sense and it *all* flew in the face of what all women in my family were taught since the first Witch.

For years I'd done so well to keep distance between us, to keep a wall up and ignore anything that hinted at any deeper feelings I might have for him. I'd seen the way he looked at me, smiled at me, the way his gaze lingered from time to time. It wasn't even a challenge to feel what he felt toward me, and yet he'd felt the meager barrier I'd put between us and for years, he'd respected it. He had never once pushed me for more or tried to seduce me into turning my back on my calling. And he could have, had he tried. Donovan was a weapon in more ways than one, and his smile was lethal. Had he even tried a little, I would have been helpless to resist him. But still, he had held back for me.

Until the end.

The memory of our kiss was a nightly recurrence. I felt his mouth on mine like a brand, a claiming. The way his hands had slid around my waist, the way his body seemed to cradle mine as we melded together as if we were two parts of the same whole *finally* put back together again. The taste of him was addictive, something spicy and exotic, and totally him. It was sinful and heavenly all at once, and nothing had ever felt quite so invigorating than sharing that kind of intimacy with him. We'd fought it all for so long, that giving in had been a euphoria I knew I'd never replicate with another. The mere idea of touching another man as I had touched Donovan or allowing myself to be touched was almost sickening to me.

The hairs on the back of my neck tingled, and a heat washed over me that I was all too familiar with.

He was here, somewhere nearby.

He never let himself be seen, he never interacted with us or made his presence known, but it was impossible for him to hide from a Witch, and especially from me. I would sense him anywhere, in any form. It was a kind of torment to know he was nearby but that I could not see him. And yet it was also somehow a soothing balm on a burn that refused to heal. Knowing he was around, whether I could see him or not, allowed me to get a sense for him and know that he was okay. I dreaded the day he stopped coming by.

My mind flashed once again to how it felt to be in his arms, held to his body, the feel of him wrapped around me...

I closed my eyes on the memory. My family had known of my last-minute weakness. They'd felt the explosion of our chemistry from buildings away. I hadn't been prepared for such a rush and in the moment, I hadn't bothered to shield us from anyone else. I'd been so wrapped up in Donovan and everything about him and the way we felt together, it had been a miracle I'd heard someone calling for me.

No one seemed to blame me for my moment of weakness.

At least as a Witch, they were able to *feel* the way I felt about him, the way I needed him and fought it. They knew the struggle I'd been through and empathized with me, but they too knew it was wrong.

But how something that felt so right could be wrong still baffled me. Even now with him hiding in the shadows somewhere in the distance, it felt right to have him nearby. He was *supposed* to be here.

I jerkily brushed my hands on my apron and pushed back the fall of hair from my face with shaky hands. The sun was hot today, making me sweat and feel tired. I should be in a good mood. I should be in high spirits because today was the celebration of Litha—the Summer Solstice—and we were making last minute preparations for the festivities that would commence an hour before the sun reached its highest peak. I should be filled with excitement and frivolity.

But I wasn't.

Blowing out a heavy breath, I realized I needed to take a break, but if I stopped, all I'd do is think about him. If I went inside to speak to my family, I would feel the way they monitored me and my emotions, as if I were a volcano threatening to erupt and they were preparing for the fallout.

Goddess above, *why was this so hard?*

"Tabitha."

I sighed at the sound of my name and slowly opened my eyes to see Bea on the other side of the garden gate once again. I should have known it would be her to find me when I was in such turmoil. In the time since I'd said goodbye to Donovan, she'd often found me in moments of deep sadness, offering her silent support. Her eyes swam with sympathy, and I detested it. I had brought this on myself, we both knew it, so I hated it when any of them looked at me like that.

"I need to take a walk," I said, pushing to my feet. I knew my emotions were draining on every Witch in the village. They could all erect barriers in their head to not feel the full extent of my emotions, but they would still feel it to some degree, and I couldn't imagine how uncomfortable I was making everyone, especially Bea. She was tied to me in a much more profound way. Maybe taking a walk would let me fortify myself enough that I could give everyone a break.

"You can't go beyond the borders of the village, we have our protection set up, remember?"

I dropped my head back on a sigh. Right. As the sense of doom I'd been feeling had become stronger in the last few days, the Wiccan Elders had agreed that we needed to start taking precautions. Without any regular humans realizing it, we'd set up a giant pentagram around the village to alert us to any evil that stepped foot inside it. Any who wished ill-will upon us or were here to cause discord would be exposed at once. We hoped this would give us an edge, a head start on evacuating our young and vulnerable, and give those of us with more power and experience in magical combat a chance to prepare.

"I still need to go," I decided.

"There are ways we can help you, Tabitha. If you would let us," Bea offered as she had done many times since Donovan left. I shook my head before she even finished speaking. She was talking about the Coven performing a spell to remove the memory of my feelings for Donovan, or about removing him entirely from my head. They wanted to help me forget, or kill the memory of my feelings for him so that I could move on and stop hurting. But the thought of it was repugnant. It felt like a betrayal, not only to myself, but to him. Donovan was a part of my life, he had been for years, and he had taken an incredibly important role in my life for that time. He didn't deserve to have the memory of him erased, or the impact he'd had. Our interactions had shaped me, and despite the pain, I refused to let myself take the easy way out.

"Are you sure?" Bea asked, a small note of exasperation in her tone.

"I know all you want to do is help me, Bea, and I understand."

"You suffer needlessly," she replied quickly, her concern genuine. I thought about her words and slowly shook my head. Donovan still stood nearby, and I could tell he worried about my wellbeing as much as my family was. He knew as well as I did that separating was for the best, but he still worried that his absence was hurting me as I was sure it was hurting him. I could not speak to him anymore, but maybe this was a chance for him to know I didn't regret the pain, no matter how bad it got.

Dragging in a slow breath, I set my shoulders and looked back at my sister, knowing Donovan was listening. "No, there is a reason

for everything, you know that, Bea. As our mother would say...
to have loved so deeply that the loss of that person is like a
physical, aching wound, is a gift you cannot perceive for many
years."

Bea sighed and I shrugged. "Many people pray to experience a
love this deep. But the consequence of experiencing such a rare
treasure is having to feel the pain of its absence once it's gone. I
know I suffer, and I hate that all of you suffer with me. But it's a
reminder of the gift I was given with Donovan, no matter how
short it lasted or how many years we tried not to feel it."

His pain was out there, as immense as mine, so it was hard to tell
where the blanket of my despair ended and his began. But I knew
he'd heard me, and I hoped that in some way, my words brought
him even the smallest measure of comfort. Slowly, the feel of
him faded, and I knew he'd gone again. He never stayed around
long anymore, and I felt it was more that he didn't trust himself
to stay and not interact if he waited around too long.

Bea sighed. "We are here, Tabitha. If ever you change your mind
and decide you cannot handle it anymore, we're all here to help
you."

I walked slowly up to the gate and wrapped my arms around my
sister, taking the small burst of comfort she pushed at me. "Thank
you, Bea."

She squeezed me tighter. "Any time."

As I pulled away, a sense of dread pulled at me, and Bea stiffened too, her eyes going wide. I pressed my hand to my stomach when I felt physically ill, and a cold sensation washed over my skin as the dread grew heavier, almost smothering.

"Tabitha?" Bea's voice shook as she said my name.

Swallowing hard, I glanced around us and noted the Witches in other gardens who were now standing still, others coming out from their houses, the same sense of dread and worry on their faces too as they all looked in the direction of town.

My hand shook as I dropped it to my side, and I knew without a doubt... whatever threat I'd felt coming these last few months... it was here.

BEFORE THE BEGINNING
A KINGS OF HELL PREQUEL NOVELLA

CHAPTER SIX

DONOVAN

"Many people pray to experience a love this deep. But the consequence of experiencing such a rare treasure is having to feel the pain of its absence once it's gone."

Tabitha's words hit me square in the chest, my heart resonating with them on a deep level. I'd never thought of pain as something to be grateful for before, but this was a new and different kind of pain. It made sense that something we felt so deeply would leave a wound that I wasn't even sure time itself would heal.

Was the pain worth what we'd had?

I barely needed the second I took to consider it before I had my answer.

Yes, absolutely. With every atom of my body the answer was yes. I wouldn't have given up anything, even knowing the pain we'd experience. Now, all that was left was to suffer the absence of it. Even if the pinnacle of our relationship had happened right at its demise, they were memories I'd never let go of.

A part of me felt soothed that she had rejected her sister's offer. I knew what Bea had been suggesting—that the Coven take away her memories or make them murky so that she felt less pain and loss. But it told me just how much she loved me that she'd rather drift in this sea of pain than lose a single second of our time together.

I shadowed to the town square to look for my brothers. I needed a drink, and at least being around them stopped me from sinking into a deeper pit of despair. I found them at a table at the tavern, drinks in hand. Malik was flirting with a pretty peasant girl who left with her head ducked and heat burning up her cheeks. That fucker would sweet talk any woman if it gave him a chance of bedding her.

"You're topside," Corvin greeted with a surprised look and a small smile as I stopped by the table.

"That's new?" I asked, cocking a brow.

"No, but a part of me expected you to be dressed in black and in mourning for the next three months or so."

I rolled my eyes. "I'm not a widower."

"Feels like you are," Devlin commented, pressing a hand to his chest. I tried harder to pull my emotions back, and Devlin shot me an apologetic look. "Sorry, brother, I was just teasing you. Don't feel like you need to go through it alone."

I shrugged. "It's my burden to bear, not yours. I don't mean for any of you to suffer alongside me."

"Don't worry about it," Cassius said, sliding a pint over to me. "Come join us."

I'd just taken a mouthful of drink when the ground beneath us rocked and rumbled violently. My brothers were on their feet in an instant and we turned to look around us. The townspeople began to shriek and scream as the buildings shook and geysers of dust and dirt spewed up all around us.

"What the fuck?" Harkyn snarled.

The air felt charged, heavy, and it was something we were all too familiar with.

"Angels," Tamas spat venomously, a sword appearing in his hand. Several Angels appeared in the sky, many more on the ground kicking in doors and breaking through walls. What the fuck was going on? But it was more than just Angels.

A blur of grey flashed quickly across my peripheral and I turned to see a creature with giant wings crash into an Angel mid-air and drive them into a building with so much force that debris flew everywhere.

"Nephilim," Adrik added with a small reservation in his voice. Honestly, the presence of the Nephilim definitely made whatever was going on a hell of a lot worse—

Tabitha.

I sucked in a sharp breath, my need to go to my woman immediate and swift. This had to be what she'd sensed coming. She'd said something was on its way, and that it scared her. What if this was it?

"Cole——" I started to tell my brother that I needed to leave when I was shoved roughly from behind. I rolled and landed on my feet again, my sword now in hand. Tamas had shoved me out of the way of an Angel Blade.

Just like that, there was no time for thought or worry, we were in a battle. Angels soared in from all over, blades flashing and teeth gnashing. Nephilim dotted the battlefield, their movements precise and deadly. I wanted to get to Tabitha and Marlee. I *needed* to get to them and make sure they were safe, but the moment I got a chance to move, I had another Angel to thwart. On and on the battle seemed to go, and I fought alongside my brothers, finding joy in letting some of my rage out. Finally, there was an outlet for all the pain I was feeling, and I made sure to channel each and every ounce of it into the fight. I don't know how long we fought before my desperation reached its limits. I needed to get the fuck outta here and get to Tabitha.

Blocking the sword of an Angel, I pushed the fucker in the chest with my foot, sending him backward several yards to land in a heap. My breath was choppy as I waited for the winged dick-bag to charge me again when Cole slid in front of me and slashed his sword through the Angel's midsection, cleanly cutting the feathery fuck in two.

Cole's glittering black eyes turned to me and he jerked his chin.

"Go to her. We feel your need. Go, we have this."

I didn't bother to express my gratitude or ask if he was sure. He wouldn't have suggested it if he didn't think they had it handled. And Tabitha needed me, I was sure of it now.

With a nod of thanks, I shadowed away from the battle, my mind on my woman.

~

TABITHA

My teeth cut into the inside of my cheek again as the fist slammed into the side of my face. The force of the punch snapped my head to the side, and I hung limply from the second Archangel's grip as he held me still while his friend punched me.

"Where are they, Witch?"

I panted and spat blood on the ground, trying not to feel the pain my body was in. The moment the Angels tripped our alarm, our village of Witches froze for a few beats and then sprung into action. The Elders and our young were gathered together, and using magic, we sent them away to our haven where we *knew* they'd be hidden and safe.

I raised my head to glare at the Archangel who'd punched me

several times, each time asking the same question.

The feel of magic in the air should have been a welcome sensation, but the two Witches who had created the psychic shield were *not* on my side, but on that of the Angels. They paid no attention to me, and instead focused on keeping us inside the shield so that I couldn't call for help.

"Where are they?" he repeated, his temper rising.

"Where are who?" I asked again, expecting another punch for my uncooperative answer.

Instead, he leaned forward and wrapped a hand around my throat and squeezed. His face was pinched with rage, making his otherwise chiseled good looks morph into something ugly. The scar along his jawline caught my attention, and I wondered what caused it. I wasn't aware that Angels or Demons scarred.

"I could snap your neck with less effort than it takes to squish a bug. I have orders to follow, and you're in my way. Now… where the *fuck* are the others?"

Breathing was a struggle, so instead I gathered the saliva and blood in my mouth and spat it at his face, causing him to release me and jerk back. My glee at seeing it hit him square in the face was short lived when the Archangel holding me punched me in the ribs. I felt something snap and I cried out, my legs trying to give out, but his hold on my arms refused to let me fall.

"You're going to regret that," the Angel snarled as he wiped my spit off his face.

"You might as well kill me," I shouted breathlessly. Panting, I raised my gaze to his and glared. "I'll never tell you what you want to know."

The Angel holding me gripped my hair and pulled hard. I cut off the cry that escaped from my lips and tried to hold back the hot tears that sprang into my eyes at the sharp sting.

"Oh, we will," he whispered against my ear. "But first, we're going to be very thorough in asking you questions. There are a *number* of things we can do to get you to talk."

I tried to shove down the icicle of fear his words invoked within me, but judging by the dark chuckle he let loose, I hadn't done it quickly enough.

Just as I was trying to fortify my mind against the torture that was to begin, a tingle started at my lower back and spread upwards, a warmth with it that was all too recognizable. My breath caught and my eyes widened as hope bloomed in my chest.

Donovan.

"Take your hands off her!"

His roar was unlike any I had heard him give before, and if I didn't know him like I did, I would have been terrified. As it was, I felt the Archangel holding me back jump sharply and I used the brief distraction to wrench from his grip with all my might.

A burst of flame shot out to where I'd just been standing, and a pain-filled scream cut through the air. I rolled to the ground and lifted my head to see Donovan hold a flame to the leader's face and throw a dagger at the one who'd held me. Another Angel appeared behind him, followed by another, and another.

Pulling on my magic, I threw the new Angels backward, hoping to give Donovan enough time. If he could just get to me, he could shadow us out of here. The other Angels were back on their feet, and more seemed to appear alongside them. There were too many.

"Donovan, hurry!" I cried, but a dagger appeared out of nowhere and slashed at him. One of the Witches watched the ongoing fight and cast her magic inward. The fire cut off abruptly with her spell, and there was a flurry of movement. The sounds of steel on steel were loud, and I scrambled backward out of the way, preparing to cast more magic, but for what? Did I give Donovan back his power? Take out the Witches? Throw the Angels as far as I could get them? I'd just raised my hands when someone grabbed my hair roughly and yanked. I cried out as I was pulled to my feet, my neck angled painfully to the side and a cold metal blade pressed against my neck.

"Demon King! I'll kill her," my captor snarled.

Donovan's eyes found me, and he hesitated. A single shivering moment hung between us where his fear for me was printed clearly on his face, and all I could do was watch it cost him his advantage. Someone slammed the handle of their sword into the back of his head, another slashed across his abdomen, and before I could even scream, he was on his knees.

"You bastard!" I glared at the Angel who appeared to be in charge, and I blanched at the sight of his melted and burned skin.

"Fuck you, Uriel," Donovan snarled, his murderous eyes pinned on the Archangel. Uriel's fist shot out so fast I didn't even see it, but I heard the snap as it collided with Donovan's face. Not once, but over and over again.

"Stop it!" I shouted, struggling against my captor, but all that did was cause him to yank harder on my hair.

Uriel gave a raspy laugh as his hand fell to his side and he looked between the two of us. "How sweet... the Witch and the Demon King. How does it feel, filth, to get between her thighs? I bet she likes it rough."

My chest heaved as I watched the fury on Donovan's face grow, and it wasn't until his gaze landed on me that I began to steady. His intense blue eyes were dark with anger and passion, but they calmed something in me.

His eyes flicked around us at the many Angels surrounding us— maybe thirty or so—before landing on me again. "*Malishka?*"

My breath hitched at his question, and I shook my head as much as I was able to. "Safe."

Relief flashed in his gaze, and I loved that his worry for my daughter was so high on his list. I shouldn't have been surprised, though. Marlee was practically his daughter too. There hadn't been an event or milestone in her life that he'd missed, and he'd been there for all the mundane things in between as well. I'd relied on him perhaps a little more than I should have, but he hadn't wanted it any other way.

Marlee was his almost as much as she was mine.

"Enough talking," Uriel snapped. My stomach protested at the sight of his burned flesh, but I managed not to throw up.

"You came to the Witch's aid, and it is obvious she means more to you than a Witch ordinarily would, so you must know where the others are," Uriel continued, turning his attention to Donovan. He tried again to rip from the grasp of the Angels holding him down, but there were too many, and I could feel the core-deep pain radiating from his stomach where the Angel Blade had slashed him. How long did he have before his wound killed him? His handsome face was carved into a scowl, pure hatred toward Uriel in his eyes.

"I don't know anything. And if I did, I still wouldn't tell you," he swore, his teeth gnashing.

Uriel smirked; his half-melted face unnatural in its waxy appearance. "Oh? So, if I were to do this…" he trailed off before pulling a small blade from his belt as he stepped closer to me. Donovan's eyes darkened, but he didn't move or say anything else. I pulled in a short, steadying breath and prepared myself for what I knew was coming.

Uriel kept his gaze on Donovan before grabbing my chin in his grip and jerking my face up. I bit back my panic and refused to look away from the burned Angel.

With a sadistic smile, he pressed the blade to the side of my face and dragged it down to my chin. White-hot pain burned across my face and I was unable to stop the strangled whimper that escaped. I could still see Donovan from the corner of my eye, and he jerked in the grasp of the Angels in a futile attempt to get to me.

Uriel grinned at Donovan's helplessness, and then with a speed I hadn't anticipated, drew the short-bladed weapon back and plunged it into my midsection. Pain lanced at me and I cried out, but it was Donovan's roar of anger that rang loudest.

Uriel laughed, the sound cold and filled with delight. "This is just the start, Donovan. We can do this for hours—days—however long it takes for you to break and tell us what we want to know. That, or we run out of places to cut and bruise on your pretty little Witch."

I raised my head, struggling to breathe, and caught Donovan's gaze. The helplessness and fury burning in his eyes gave me strength and I forced myself to get a handle on my breathing.

I shook my head. "There's nothing you can tell them. You don't know anything."

It was the truth. As much as I trusted him, as much as I loved him, he'd never been privy to the Witch's Haven, and it was that way on purpose.

Donovan's face hardened as I could see the wheels in his head turning. If he didn't tell them what they wanted to know, they would continue to torture me. His arms were being held outstretched, each one restrained by two Angels, several more held back the rest of him. There were at least thirty Angels surrounding us, and the two Witches working the psychic shield so he couldn't call for his brothers.

It was just us here, and there was no way out. I was going to die. The reality of those words finally sank home, and my breath left in a jerky rush. I didn't want to die, and definitely not at the hands of these Angels, but at least my family were safe, at least Marlee would be safe. I just wished Donovan wasn't here to witness it.

"Stop," Donovan ordered sharply, and when my vision focused again, I could see he was talking to me. As always, he seemed to be able to read me well enough to know what I was thinking.

"Tell us what we want to know, Demon King, or watch her die. The choice is yours," Uriel demanded once more, his tone lighter.

"He doesn't know anything," I said again, speaking directly to Uriel this time.

"I don't believe you," Uriel shot back.

"Why would we tell a Demon King the location of the other

Witches? What sense is there in that?"

Uriel pressed the tip of the blade beneath my chin, his face inching closer to mine. "What sense is there in a Witch who fucks around with a Demon King? What does it say about you and your family that you're consorting with *his* kind?"

"Maybe that we're smart enough not to be brainwashed by yours," I returned, my voice shaking.

Uriel's smile was slow and vicious, and I tried to repress the shiver that worked its way down my spine as he slid the tip of the blade down my throat to my chest.

"Then I guess torturing *you* for the information will have to do. The Demon King bearing witness will just be a pleasurable and unexpected gift."

"Uriel—" Donovan started, but my scream cut off whatever else he said when Uriel dragged the blade upwards and across my chest to my shoulder, leaving behind a long cut. The burning was instant and brought tears to my eyes, but I could handle the pain... for now.

"So, Witch. Where are the others?"

"As if I would tell you," I replied with a pant, glaring up at him. He grinned again, as if my answer was exactly what he'd hoped for. Readjusting his grip on the blade, Uriel gripped the bottom of my shirt and tore away the material, bearing my midsection and the small wound already there.

"You'll talk... eventually they all do. It's up to you how painful things get first."

I slid my gaze to Donovan who watched with wide, furious eyes, his fear for me bright and burning.

Swallowing hard, I sent him a small nod. "I can take it."

Uriel laughed and leaned in closer, the tip of the blade pressing hard against my stomach. "We'll see."

Then he plunged the blade into me.

~

DONOVAN

It felt like an eternity, but couldn't have been longer than an hour that Uriel continued to torture Tabitha while I could do nothing but watch.

I was outnumbered, restrained, and due to the barrier of magic I could feel overhead, I could not even reach out to my brothers for aid. We were alone here, and I knew that the war raging in town would keep my brothers distracted long enough that they would not think to look for me for a while.

Tabitha's scream brought me back to the scene before us, and I gritted my teeth against the furious rage I wanted to bellow. I was fucking useless right now, and being forced to watch them torture the woman I loved was a fate worse than death. My only relief was that Marlee wasn't here. The others must have gotten out, but why hadn't Tabitha?

Uriel sighed dramatically and jerked his head at the Angel holding Tabitha on her feet. Her skin was smeared with blood, and I could feel the throbbing pain she suffered.

"Put her down," Uriel ordered, and I snarled a warning at the Angel when he shoved Tabitha toward me so that she landed in a heap a few feet away.

I can take it.

Her whispered words had filled me with equal parts dread and pride. I knew my Witch was strong, stronger than anyone I had met before, and she had *every* reason to keep the location of the other Witches a secret. I knew the torture Angels were capable of, and I was near certain there was nothing they could do to her that would make her reveal their location, not when Marlee was with them.

"Tabitha?" I whispered, needing to see her move, to hear her voice, to know she could still fight.

"I think..." she trailed off and shakily pushed herself up so she was braced on her elbows. "I think I always knew what side I was on in this ongoing war between your two kinds," she continued with a wince. "This just confirmed it."

My lips trembled with her attempt at humor and I fought the hands still gripping my arms and holding me captive. There wasn't even the smallest bit of give, and whatever the Witches were doing was hindering my ability to draw on hellfire.

Fuck.

"You need to use your magic and get out of here. Go somewhere, anywhere. Find my brothers," I whispered desperately, watching Uriel talk to another Archangel as they studied her house.

"And leave you?"

My heart turned over as those beautiful eyes of hers rose to meet mine, and I wanted nothing more than to get her somewhere safe, somewhere nothing could hurt her ever again.

"They're really safe?" I whispered, almost inaudibly, needing to know Marlee would never be subjected to this kind of pain.

She nodded, the relief in her eyes matching mine.

"Alright, time is up," Uriel said, turning back to us. "We have other avenues to pursue, it's not worth keeping you around."

I barely had time to process what he meant when Tabitha moved quickly, pressing her bloody hands to my face and pressing her lips to mine in a desperate kiss. There was a finality to her touch, a farewell, and knowing that kept me momentarily paralyzed.

She pulled away slightly, eyes swimming with tears and hands holding my face so I remained looking at her.

"Audi verba mea," she whispered, pushing her magic at me. I felt the power it took from her, the effort she had to exude considering the powerful fortress the other two Witches had

constructed, but somehow her spell got through. I felt the zap of power shock through me, and a faint, brittle pathway opened up in my mind.

But before I could do more than acknowledge that it was there, Uriel was on her. She cried out as he roughly pulled her to her feet and I pulled harder on the hands restraining me.

"Say goodbye, Demon King."

"Uriel, don't!"

My words were pointless though, when he drew a new dagger from his belt, this one far larger than the one he'd previously used. With a gleeful expression, Uriel stared at me as he drove the dagger down, burying it in Tabitha's body.

"Tabitha!

Her name ripped up my throat, from somewhere deep inside me, and her pain hit me like a volcanic blast. My vision narrowed so that I only saw her, only saw the pain on her face, and the devastating knowledge that this was the end for her.

The end for us.

CHAPTER SEVEN

DONOVAN

"Tabitha!"

No sound escaped her lips as her wide eyes found mine, pain and tears shining back at me.

"No!" I roared and fought harder to get to her. The grip on one of my arms loosened and I threw everything into getting away, struggling harder, fighting beyond the pain of the Angel Blade wound across my abdomen to get to the woman I loved. But as one Angel lost their grip on me, another took their place, and soon I was being held down by more of them, watching helplessly as Uriel dragged Tabitha's limp form toward her home.

"You fucking bastards! I will end you for this, I will hunt you down and wring every ounce of pain you are capable of feeling from your body before I let you die!"

Uriel didn't bother to respond and I watched him disappear inside the home with Tabitha and reappear a few seconds later… without her.

What the fuck were they doing?

"Donovan?"

My breath caught at the faint stirring of consciousness in my mind, and I recognized Tabitha's touch at once.

"Moya lyubov'," I whispered, feeling my love for her burst over at the feel of her in my head. I didn't care how she'd been able to forge a psychic connection between us, only that I could reach her now.

"You have to know that I never wanted to lose you, Donovan. I never wanted to be away from you," she whispered, and even now I could hear the tears in her voice.

"I know, moya lyubov'. I know why we were apart," I hurried to reassure, even as I continued to struggle against my captors.

"Donovan…" she trailed off as pain lanced through her again, her injuries harder to ignore. I forced myself further into her head to take her pain, better equipped to ignore such a thing.

"You need to get up, Tabitha. I will take your pain; you need to move. Run now, while you can, while they think you are too injured."

I felt her shake her head, the denial already there. *"He has me bound to a chair. I cannot escape, even if I had the energy or power to run."*

Despair washed over me again and I gritted my teeth against the need to roar. Uriel was smirking as he talked to another Angel, drawing out Tabitha's pain and my helplessness.

"Donovan… I don't have any more time. I am fading. But I need you to

know... I... I was always yours. From the moment we met, you claimed a piece of me, and over time you've taken ownership of my whole heart. You are Marlee's father, her best friend, and I am so grateful you were there in her life... and in mine."

I shook my head and tried to push back the burning in my eyes. *"Don't... moya lyubov', don't give up. Fight."*

"I have no more fight, Donovan. Marlee is safe, my family are safe and will look after her. They will make sure she knows she was loved fiercely and completely. My time ends here, with the love of my life to help ease my journey to the other side."

Closing my eyes, I tried to find the words to encourage her to keep fighting when there was a sudden whoosh of sound. I opened my eyes to find Tabitha's house engulfed in flames... with her trapped inside.

I bellowed my rage and denial, tugging with all my might against the Angels with reserves of power I did not know I had. My arms slid free and I wasted no time in slashing out against those nearest. Yanking a blade from one of their belts, I threw it at the nearest Witch, watching with satisfaction as it skewered her through the neck. She choked, stumbled, and fell lifeless. With her dead, the psychic shield shattered and my control of hellfire came back.

Spinning quickly, I raised my hand and felt for the fire engulfing the house, all the while feeling Tabitha slip further and further away. Blood loss was already a massive threat, and the smoke had reached her. Breathing was a tremendous task, and I knew I had seconds before she was too far gone. I'd just gotten a feel for the flames when power hit me square in the chest forcing me to let go of the fire. I flew back several feet and slammed into the unforgiving ground, pain shooting through me with sharp stabs. My breath stalled for several seconds, but I was up in less time. Nothing was going to stop me from reaching Tabitha.

I threw my arm wide to engulf the nearby Angels with more hellfire, keeping them at bay and picked up another bladed weapon from the ground, throwing it at the Witch who had just thrown me into the air. She deflected it easily, her dark eyes revealing her deep hatred of my kind.

Using my other hand, I directed a jet of hellfire her way, but she kept herself well protected. I was just about to double-down when a dagger hit me out of nowhere, embedding itself up to the hilt in my shoulder. Uriel appeared out of nowhere, his fist slamming into my face and sending me flying again.

"Donovan?"

Tabitha... her voice was weak, listless. She had moments left.

"I am coming, moya lyubov'. Please, stay... fight," I urged, rolling to evade Uriel's booted foot. I rolled again and pushed to my feet, yanking the dagger from my shoulder and throwing it back at him. He hissed as it found its mark in his gut and I rushed him. Before I could make contact, power wrapped around me and

slammed me down onto my knees. It was like a vice, holding my arms to my side and squeezing tight, refusing to let me go. There was no room, no give, there was no way out. Uriel turned me to face the house engulfed in flames, his victorious smirk enough to make me want to tear him to shreds where he stood. But I was helpless, hopeless. I gave a wordless roar and reached for my brothers, glad to find the psychic barrier well and truly gone.

"Help me, brothers! I have need of you!"

The shock that went through our lines of connection was enormous, but I could not concentrate long enough to explain things to them or to plead.

Tabitha was slipping away.

"We are coming brother, hold on," Cassius replied, and I could feel his great wounds and the fight that kept him away.

"Moya lyubov', stay with me," I pleaded. She barely held on; her pain too great even with me taking much of the load. Her lifeblood continued to seep away from her, and her lungs burned and body felt heavy.

"I will take the memory of you into my next life, and every life after that in the hopes that you will find me there. I will live on; my soul will remain the same. Come find me, Donovan. Look for me in another life and we can have what we should have had in this one."

My eyes burned and I closed my eyes as defeat began to weigh down on me. I didn't want to admit that she was right, but there was no choice, nowhere for her to go, no way for me to get to her.

Dragging in a breath, I closed my eyes and wrapped myself around her, pulling her close and enveloping her with every ounce of my love, even as my heart broke and my soul wailed.

She wept silently, and I knew she was scared, that she was in pain even though I'd taken a great deal from her already.

I concentrated on taking more from her, determined to make her passing as peaceful as possible. Because this was the end.

Opening myself up fully to her, I brought her into a memory of us.

It was a late summer afternoon. Marlee, Tabitha, and I were in the forest as we often were. The sun filtered through the canopy, sending shards of golden light shining down on us.

Marlee ran ahead of us, her beautiful curls bouncing, her insanely heart-melting giggle echoing around me.

It was one of my favorite memories. We had been happy, content, in a world of our own for one afternoon. Anything had seemed possible; everything had seemed within our grasp.

I walked beside Tabitha as I had done that afternoon, but this time, I reached over to tangle our fingers together. She turned and looked up at me in surprise, her stunning eyes bright and wide. A heartbeat passed, and a smile curved her lips, the one that made my entire body light up in awe.

"I never should have kept you at arm's length," she whispered, slowing us to a stop so she could face me more fully.

"I would not change a thing about our time together, Tabitha. It was as it was meant to be," I assured, tilting my head as her hand came up to cup my cheek.

"But we missed out on so much," she whispered, tears glistening in her eyes. I shook my head and leaned closer, pressing my forehead to hers.

"We gained so much, too. I never could have imagined such beauty for myself. You and Marlee gave me joy and love unlike anything I ever knew I could experience. I'll carry that with me for always," I assured her, needing her to focus on the positive.

"You were such an amazing father, Donovan. Marlee is an incredibly lucky girl to have known your love and protection," she whispered. Her words were like a knife being driven into my heart, and every word twisted it painfully.

She flinched and for a moment the color of our dream-world flickered dangerously as her injuries tried to snatch her away too soon.

"Hey," I whispered and tilted her head up to look at me, pain lancing through me at knowing that her body was burning at this very moment. She was almost gone. I forced a smile on my face, however, determined to protect her last moments from the ugliness of reality. "Focus on me, on this. Focus on what we have here, on this amazing day we shared," I encouraged as Marlee came running back.

"Come on, Doni. Mama and I planted flowers in the garden, come look!"

Tabitha's face brightened as she peered down at her daughter before she smiled back at me, love and warmth shining radiantly. I wanted to reach down and hug Marlee, to hold her one more time, to tell her how much I loved her. But this was a memory, not a psychic realm. Tabitha and I could change things with each other because we were both here in the memory, but Marlee was not.

"Come on, Mama!" Marlee called, letting go of my hand to take her mother's.

Tabitha looked up at me again and I leaned forward to kiss her, wishing we had more time, wishing I could say everything I needed to say, but there was no time.

Her lips clung to mine as I pulled back, and I paused before raising my head, soaking in the warmth of her, the love shining from her depths. The words were never spoken, nor would they ever be. But here and now, in this moment, I felt her love, and it was a memory I wanted to cherish forever.

"Go on, *lyubov'*, your daughter is calling for you," I whispered, letting my hand fall from her face.

Her eyes shone with tears and the smile on her lips trembled as fear of the unknown tried to engulf her.

"Will you come find me?" she whispered.

"Nothing short of death will stop me from finding you again, *moya lyubov'*. I will look for you in this life and the next, and all the ones that follow."

Nodding jerkily, Tabitha shone that brilliant smile of hers my way once more before she let her daughter pull her away. I released her hand, her fingers sliding from mine, and I watched with a heavy heart as Marlee and Tabitha walked away from me.

And with them, I felt Tabitha's spirit disappear.

I fell back into my own body, and the pain of my injuries were numb compared to the pain of losing Tabitha. When I opened my eyes, they were wet, and I could no longer feel Tabitha's life force.

She was gone.

My breath came choppy and rough, and when I locked my eyes on Uriel again, it was with every cell of hatred I possessed.

"You have signed your own name upon Death's Scroll this day, Uriel," I ground out, my body vibrating with pent-up fury. "It does not matter where you go, where you hide, or what you do to protect yourself. You *will* die by my hand, and your suffering shall exceed anything you could anticipate."

Uriel's smile faltered slightly, and I watched him lift his chin and set his jaw. "You will not live past this day, Demon King. Your threats are empty."

He raised his sword to press against my neck, eyes promising death.

There was a rush of wind from somewhere to my right, followed by another on my left. I flicked my attention to the side in time to see the Witch's head jerk sharply and her neck snap. Uriel's sword drifted away from my neck in surprise as she fell lifelessly to the ground to reveal the bloody and injured form of Tamas, his expression murderous. "I beg to differ, fuckface."

A beat of silence, and then chaos broke out. Several of my brothers appeared, all as bloody and injured as each other, further evidence of the war they'd already waged. At their appearance, Angels burst into action all around. With the death of the last Witch, the bonds that held me were gone, and I climbed to my feet. The Angel Blade wound along my abdomen wrenched at me, but I ignored it and forced myself to my feet, my gaze on Uriel as I withdrew my sword. "Now, what were you saying?"

Uriel raised his sword, but before I could even charge at him, the fucking coward disappeared in a whoosh of air and a flash of pale grey wings.

"Coward!" I shouted thunderously.

There was no time to rage, however, as more Angels poured in from everywhere. With fire and blades, we fought the garrison of Angels determined to kill us. But with every Angel I killed, it was Uriel's face I saw, his smug smile as he tortured Tabitha and drew every scream from her. With every strike of my blade, I took my revenge, hearing her cries, feeling her hopelessness. Flashes of her bright smile lit up inside my mind, and the pain of losing her all over again built and built.

I thought I had exhausted all sorrow and rage. I fought so long and so hard that I was surprised when more Angels kept coming, but I did not stop, I could not stop.

The fury that lived inside me was growing, feeding, needing more death, more carnage. The need was so powerful it was consuming me from the inside. Somehow, I could feel it radiating out, as if I were encompassing all the pain and turmoil around me and it was becoming something… more.

"Donovan!" That was Cole, but he sounded far away.

"What's he doing?" Tamas shouted, his voice bouncing around, coming in and out of focus.

"Donovan, stop!" Cassius this time, but his voice was also coming from a great distance.

The rage built and churned, turning into something unmanageable, impossible to confine or control. Heat scorched through me, so forcefully I could barely breathe. I was a vessel now, a conduit, nothing more than a means with which to ignite the powder-keg of wrath that was amassing within me.

"Fuck, he's lost." Adrik cursed.

"What do we do?" Harkyn asked with a grunt.

"Don't let him go. Hold on and get low!" Malik shouted.

I couldn't see anything anymore, could barely hear. My ears were ringing and I was searing hot to my very core. I could barely catch my breath as the wind whipped around me getting faster and faster, the well of fury within me seemingly never-ending. I knew it was mine, but it wasn't *just* mine. There was more than my anguish here, but mixed together and in need of an outlet, it was somehow being channeled through me.

I felt my brothers, not physically, but in my mind. They were surrounding me, grounding me, keeping me close in an effort to keep the pieces of me together as the tempest of fury raged through me in the form of a storm so powerful, I wasn't sure any of us would survive it. I tried to warn them, I tried to tell them to run, to save themselves while they had the chance, but the words barely formed in my mind and refused to spill from my lips.

Echoes of Tabitha's laughter and Marlee's giggles whipped around us. The sounds of other people—women, children, family and friends—they all resonated in a never-ending loop as the storm built and built, the summit of it ever closer.

"*Donovan!*"

My name was barely discernible over the ruthless storm and then...

Everything exploded.

The storm within me burst forth, relentless and unforgiving. My arms flew wide at my side and a blinding light shot forth. The wind that had whipped around me was hot and powerful, a wave of destruction demolishing everything in its wake.

BEFORE THE BEGINNING
A KINGS OF HELL PREQUEL NOVELLA

CHAPTER EIGHT

DONOVAN

I remained on my knees in the aftermath of the destruction I'd wrought.

I didn't understand magic enough to know how I'd done what I'd done, only that it had happened. *Exhausted* didn't even begin to cover how I felt. A perpetual dust seemed to hang in the air in the aftershock of our battle, it was so thick the late afternoon sun was struggling to penetrate it.

I was kneeling in the center of the explosion. The surrounding trees were wiped out, laid flat as if they had been blown back from the force of the wind. There were no buildings in sight, everything had turned to rubble.

My brothers were okay. I had worried the explosion would kill them, but they were still there, whole and unharmed by what I'd done. After bringing a Witch over to heal the Angel Blade wounds I'd suffered, they stayed by my side for a long while, trying to console me. But after recognizing they would not get a response from me, they left me to my despair. I knew they were nothing but a call away, but I needed to be alone.

Tabitha was gone.

She was gone, and there was nothing I could do to bring her back. I'd been filled with such certainty that I could save her, that the Angels wouldn't win, that I'd hold her in my arms again and take her back to Marlee. I was a King of Hell. I had power beyond what most beings could fathom, and when I wanted a particular outcome, I got it. It had been that way for so long that the possibility of losing hadn't *actually* seemed to be a real possibility, not deep down. But I'd been wrong. The Angels had won, and to make matters worse, Uriel had gotten away.

I wanted to be angry while thinking his name, but I was empty, utterly spent. Whatever I'd done to cause such devastation had taken all reserves of energy from me.

At the sound of approaching footsteps, I didn't even bother to look up. I didn't care if it was friend or foe, my will to do anything was nil. Whoever was approaching stopped beside me, and with a glance at the shoes, I could tell it was a woman.

She sniffled and slowly knelt beside me, her hand coming to rest on my shoulder.

"You did the best you could, Donovan."

Her voice was a shard of glass to my heart, the first thing I'd felt in hours, and I slowly raised my gaze to meet her ravaged expression.

Bea.

She and Tabitha weren't identical twins, but they looked enough alike that seeing her now hurt on a level I wasn't expecting so soon after nearly burning myself out completely.

"I failed her," I whispered, my voice a rasp of sound.

Bea shook her head and placed both hands on my shoulders, tears spilling onto her cheeks. "No, you were there for her in a way none of us could be. Without you, her death would have been so much more painful. I was connected to her in the end, and I experienced what she felt. She was content, at peace, happy. She was sad too, yes, but compared to how it could have gone… Donovan, you did everything you could."

My eyes burned, and I ducked my head as grief began to overwhelm me again. I wasn't sure I could survive this. The feeling in my chest, the sudden emptiness in my soul that Tabitha's absence had caused… it was a yawning chasm of despair that threatened to swallow me whole.

"Why did she stay?" I asked, forcing the words past the lump in my throat. "When you all left for safety, why did she stay?"

Bea didn't reply right away, and when I raised my gaze to look at her again, the answer was there in her grief-stricken face.

"No," I whispered, denial ripping through me. "No… she…" I struggled to speak.

"Donovan—"

"She stayed for me?" I asked, forcing the words out. "She stayed because she was worried about me?"

Another tear broke free to track down Bea's cheek and she swiped at it with the back of her hand. "Tabitha loved you, Donovan. She loved you *so* deeply, as much as you loved her. She could never have abandoned you if she thought there was a chance you were in danger."

"Why didn't anyone make her go? Why didn't *you*? I'm a Demon King; I would have been fine. But she——" my voice cracked and guilt ripped through me. She'd stayed for *me*.

"You knew Tabitha as well as any of us. Do you really think anyone could have made her do something she didn't want to do?"

I lifted the heels of my palms to my eyes and pressed hard as I began to rock back and forth. No, no, no. This couldn't be happening.

"The others are safe. Marlee is safe," Bea continued, her voice thick with tears. "She knows her mama isn't coming back, and she is sad about that. But she has all of us to help get her through it, and she's safe."

Her words soothed something inside me, knowing Marlee was safe. I wanted nothing more than to wrap my little girl up in my arms and hold her tight, but saying goodbye to her once had damn near ruined me. I couldn't go through it again, not now when Tabitha was gone for good.

"Your training saved us. It saved a lot of the girls. They were fast to react, to listen to our warnings. They used their skills and for those who weren't so quick, there were more of us capable of picking up the slack. You're the reason we all made it out, Donovan."

Everyone except Tabitha.

No one said it, but the words were there nonetheless.

"I can't do this, Bea. I don't know how I'm meant to keep going without her, knowing that she's not..." my words failed as the reality of my future set in.

Bea was silent a long moment before she gently cupped my face and raised my head so I had to look at her.

"There is something I can do for you, Donovan. It will help you move on."

Her words echoed what she'd told Tabitha earlier and I shook my head. "I don't want to forget."

"Not forget," she hurried to say. "Just... distance you from it. Make the memories a little hazy, the emotions a little less intense."

"I..." I shook my head, hating the idea of it.

"Donovan," she said gently. "Look around. Look at what your grief did. What happens if you lose control again?"

"How did I do this? I don't even know what happened," I admitted.

She hesitated and sighed. "It wasn't just your grief you felt.

119

Somehow, you tapped into another source of grief, and after the events of today, it is not surprising there was so much of it to feel. When it all melded together, it did this," she explained.

Another source? I wanted to know more, but I shook my head, my ability to think on things so complex was limited right now, and I had other things to consider.

Bea was right, I knew she was, and really… what did I have to lose by lessening the intensity of what I was feeling? Tabitha was gone for good, and I was left here trying to carry on.

"It feels like I'm betraying her," I admitted.

Bea nodded slowly, understanding bright in her sad eyes. "There is another reason I need to distance you from your emotions and make your memories hazy, Donovan."

I watched her, my brain slow to clue in as the cogs in my head turned sluggishly. The answer came to me though, and I couldn't find it in myself to be fired up over it.

"You are all going into hiding, and you don't want me to know half of what I know," I said aloud.

"We trust you, Donovan. We would not have allowed your presence in our village or for you to be alone with our children if we did not trust you. But today proved that times are changing, that things are getting worse for the future of Witches, and we need to protect ourselves."

I couldn't even argue with her, because she was right. Usually,

Angels and Demons could agree on one thing: that humans are not to be given proof of divinity. We all kept ourselves hidden and shadowed in order to keep the balance and remain undetected. But today, the Angels had broken that rule on a massive scale in what I could now tell was an attempt to take more than one Coven at once. They had tortured Tabitha for the location of the Witches who had escaped, and they hadn't seemed to care that humans saw them, or the destruction they caused while they attempted to keep the rest of us distracted in the village.

The Angels were up to something, and it was clear Witches were the desired prize. I would die before revealing anything about Marlee or her family, but I could understand why they wanted assurances that I couldn't accidentally let something slip.

"Will you take everything?" I asked hoarsely.

Bea shook her head and dropped her hands. "No. I never want to take her away from you, she lives on in your mind as long as you remember her. But I will lessen your grief slightly and… and alter some of what you know."

I frowned. "Alter how?"

She let out a long breath. "I have a memory prepared, one with another ending to what happened here tonight. You will think that we all died, that you arrived to help Tabitha as you did, but that her family were being held inside the house. When they…" she paused and took a moment to steady herself. "When they took Tabitha inside, they set fire to it, but we were *all* inside."

My eyes widened slightly. "Even Marlee?"

Her eyes shone with tears and she nodded. "All of us. We need you to think we're all gone so that you don't one day come looking for us and accidentally put us at risk. We need to know we're safe."

I was shaking my head. "How will thinking you all died— thinking Marlee died—ease my grief?"

She ducked her head and took a moment to meet my gaze again. "We want to remove any memories of Marlee. As far as you'll remember, you and Tabitha were fantastic friends, and yes, you helped some of our children hone their skills, but Marlee wasn't a part of it. She is a big part of your grief, and if we can erase her from your head, it will help."

My head was spinning, denial lodging in the forefront of my mind, but there was this voice deeper down, one that told me this would be best for everyone. Even if I remembered Marlee, I'd never see her again, I already knew that. She was safer away from me and everything to do with this world... it would protect her indefinitely if she was removed from my mind as well. I could not be tempted to go looking for her. It killed to know that I would no longer have memories of her to call on when I needed her comfort, but it would be as if she never existed. And as for the rest of her idea, the altered memory that told me they'd all died… it was the same for them all.

If everyone thought they'd all died, everyone would be safer.

I closed my eyes and forced myself to breathe, to accept this new idea because I already knew it was for the best, even if I didn't like it. It would work, too, because no one outside of Tabitha's family knew of my attachment to Marlee. My brothers knew I trained some of the young Witches, but I'd never told them of my role in Marlee's life. I'd wanted to be sure no one could use her against me. Demons could be assholes, after all, even if I knew my brothers would never hurt me that way. It didn't mean none of those they ruled would not discover my attachment to the girl.

"Many people pray to experience a love this deep. But the consequence of experiencing such a rare treasure is having to feel the pain of its absence once it's gone." I whispered the words I'd heard Tabitha say not too long ago, and Bea stiffened. Her eyes filled with tears once more and her lips trembled.

"For humans and the rest of us with a shorter lifespan, yes. But for a being such as yourself, perhaps the consequence is never having a memory of having it at all."

That burning, aching whirlpool of grief was tugging at me again, making everything cloudy and chaotic. Everything hurt, it hurt so much. "I made her a promise, Bea. I told her I would carry her memory with me, that I'd find her again one day. Her soul will be the same, and maybe in another life we'd be together."

"And you can keep your promise," she assured, wiping at the wetness on her face. "I will not take Tabitha from you. You have my word. I want her in your memories because then this version of her soul lives on forever. But I will lessen the grief, perhaps dull your feelings slightly so that you have a chance of moving on."

I hated it... but I could feel the need for destruction rising, even as we spoke. I hurt so much and I wanted to cause it to everything in my wake so that others would feel it too. I didn't want to be this way. Acting like that was *not* who I was, but losing Tabitha had warped something inside me, and I wasn't sure I would be capable of being myself again if I started down this path.

"I need to protect my family, Donovan. I need to protect Marlee. Can you understand that?"

"Of course I can," I answered quickly, and I realized how true I knew those words to be. She had to protect them now, not me. I needed to step back, to let them live their lives without me around, and I had to trust that they all knew enough to keep safe and hidden. Bea loved Marlee like her own children, she would move heaven and earth to keep her safe, especially now that Tabitha wasn't here to do it.

"Can you tell Marlee something for me?" I asked, wanting her to know I didn't abandon her.

Bea hesitated and nodded, her words cautious. "I *can*."

"*Will* you pass on a message from me? I don't want her to think I left her too."

Bea's eyes were wet as she nodded and she tried to smile. "I can do that."

Dragging in a shaky breath, I nodded and scrubbed my hands over my face. "Please tell her that I love her, that I will *always* love her. My little *Malishka*. Tell her how proud of her I am, how I know she will grow into a beautiful, kind, and powerful Witch who will protect her people and save so many lives."

Bea's eyes shone, and I pushed on, trying to find the words. "Tell her that it's okay to miss her mother, that we'll both miss and love her forever. Let her know I'll be looking over her, even if she can't feel me, I'm there. Make sure she knows she was so loved, and that I will love her forever. Will you tell her that, please? I don't want her to feel like I abandoned her." The pain was beginning to overwhelm me once again. I didn't think I was at risk of detonating like I had done before, but I was still unpredictable in this state, and likely would be for a long time.

"I'll tell her, Donovan. I promise."

Nodding, I swallowed hard and gritted my teeth. "Do it." I knew if she didn't do it now, I'd never let her close enough to do it again, and I'd go looking for Marlee in order to ease some of my grief.

Bea drew in a shaky breath and gently placed her hands on either side of my head once more. I struggled to take a breath and waited as she centered herself. My heart broke as I let her into my head, but her presence acted as a soothing balm on a blistering burn. No, it didn't heal, but the initial and unbearable pain was already lessening so I could think rationally. She started at the end, at the dream I'd conjured for Tabitha and removed Marlee. The intensity of the dream was lessened only slightly, and then she was onto Tabitha's death.

I felt Bea's devastation at feeling her sister's death again and at feeling it from my point of view. Raising my hands, I gently gripped her wrists in an attempt to steady her, and Bea took in another choppy breath, her appreciation obvious now that she was in my head.

I forced myself to stay open to her as she moved through my memories of her sister and carefully removed Marlee in each one. As she left each memory, I felt my grief lessen in small increments every time, but I knew no matter what she did, I would not be okay for a long time. It was strange having memories removed, but felt stranger still at having a manufactured memory placed in my mind. My initial reaction was to fight it, to push it out and close down, but at Bea's instruction, I breathed through it and let her do what had to be done.

Things went hazy, fuzzy, and having a real thought was a

struggle. I felt as though I were moving through molasses and that my whole body had pins and needles. I tried to form a thought, but before I could grasp it, it would disappear on me. Before I knew it, I'd waded my way into darkness, something warm and peaceful, something I desperately ached for. My mind felt tired, stretched to its limits.

"Goodbye, Donovan."

The words were a mere whisper on the wind, barely tangible, but I felt them sweep over me before the safety of darkness pulled me under.

~

I woke with a start on the ground surrounded by cool night air. It took me a few seconds to orient myself, my head fuzzy, and when I finally did, it all came rushing back.

Tabitha was dead.

Her whole family was dead.

I closed my eyes on the pain and guilt that assailed me and fought through the agony of knowing I'd failed her—failed *them*. The area around me was still decimated, a crater where Tabitha's house and those of the other Witch's had once stood. Everything was gone now.

Forcing myself to my feet, I looked around a little numbly. What was I meant to do now? How did I move on from such a loss? I ground my teeth and tried to push the anguish aside. Fuck, this was why we didn't get attached to anyone, this was why we kept space between us and humans. I couldn't imagine going through this every few decades, losing friends and lovers to their own mortality.

Caring for my brothers was enough, they were the only safe option.

Closing my eyes, I reached for that switch in the back of my head and wrapped myself in shadow before traveling back to Hell.

My feet touched down on the marble floor, and I looked around desolately. I had duties as a King of Hell I could not ignore, things that needed tending, but everything seemed like a nuisance right now, a burden.

"You're back," Cassius greeted as he strode down the Hall.

"I am," I answered stiffly.

"Can I do anything for you?" he asked a little awkwardly.

I ducked my head and shook it. "No."

When silence fell between us again, I decided it was time to go to my realm, but before I could, there was a whoosh and a snarling sound that had the hairs on the back of my neck standing on end. I turned to my left to see Devlin glowering at Corvin before shoving him toward the hall.

"Go. *Now*."

"*Fuck* you," Corvin snapped, his expression nearly feral. Despite my own ocean of melancholy and grief, I was surprised at the deadly look on my brother's face. What the hell had happened? Corvin was never like this. Confusion flooded me as I stared wondering what was going on.

"You asked for my help, so you're getting it. I have your Token and I'll keep calling your ass back home if you don't stay here on your own. You can make this as difficult as you want, or you can just go to your realm and stay there."

At the look on Corvin's face, I took a single, sliding step backward, a very real shiver of fear working its way up my spine. Cassius had stopped breathing as we watched the scene before us. Something was *very* wrong.

Corvin and Devlin faced off against one another, both unmovable forces about to go head-to-head. The air became thick with tension and crackled with suppressed rage and power, but no one moved.

"Dev—"

"I made you a promise, Corvin. Now *move*," Devlin cut in, his tone low and furious. What promise?

For a moment, I didn't think Corvin was going to listen, but with a snarl of disdain, he spun on his heel and marched with furious steps to his realm, the door slamming shut behind him.

Cassius and I turned to look at each other with wide eyes, but I was too fucking tired to dwell on whatever the hell that was for too long.

"What's going on?" Cassius asked Devlin.

Our brother's gaze swung to us and lingered on me, sympathy shining in his eyes.

"I'm sorry for your loss, Donovan," he murmured, looking bone weary.

"Haven't you heard?" Cassius asked with a lame attempt at smiling. "His name is Nova now. As in, *Supernova*. The crater he left in the ground was seriously impressive."

Devlin looked at me with curious eyes, something in his expression setting off alarm bells, but again, everything felt like mush in my head and I couldn't give it any real consideration.

"Is Corvin okay?" I asked, my voice hoarse.

Devlin's expression turned cagey and he ducked his head and shook it as he studied Corvin's Token in his hand. "Not even a little bit. Do him and yourself a favor, yeah? Keep out of his way for a while… a long while. And don't call on him unless it's life or death."

I frowned. "Why?"

He hesitated and sighed before looking at me with sad eyes.

"You're not the only one who suffered tonight. I suggest you take some time alone as well, as much as you need. The rest of us will handle any slack that needs picking up."

Curiosity for whatever Corvin was going through tugged at me, but it was overshadowed by the relief and gratitude I felt at Devlin's offer.

"Thank you, brother. I think I'm going to do just that," I replied, taking a few steps toward my realm. I turned to look at Cassius and sighed. "I'm glad all of you are okay. Thank you for coming to me as soon as you could."

Cassius's expression twisted into one of regret. "Sorry it wasn't soon enough, brother."

I nodded jerkily and cleared my throat before turning away and starting toward my door. I wasn't sure what the future held anymore, but it seemed a whole hell of a lot duller without my best friend in it.

BEFORE THE BEGINNING
A KINGS OF HELL PREQUEL NOVELLA

EPILOGUE

DONOVAN

A few hundred years later...

"Can I see her yet?" I asked Cole, pacing in the Hall with my book in hand as I waited for my brother to respond. I understood that he'd gone through something terrible and that having Tomika alive again was a damn miracle, but if he could just take an hour from fucking her brains out, I might actually be able to get to the bottom of a theory I'd had since the moment I laid eyes on her. Witches were back.

The knowledge still rocked me, and it lit a fire inside me, something I hadn't felt in centuries. Not only was there a real-life Witch here in Hell with us, but she was a Wardwell descendent. She was a descendant of Tabitha's, and that meant someone had lived, someone had survived the massacre. I wasn't sure who it was, but it filled me with a sense of relief and a deep sense of purpose to know it had happened.

I had a duty to fulfill. I'd promised Tabitha a long time ago that I would protect her family, that I would always be there for them. Thinking I'd failed completely these last few hundred years had been a weight that no amount of Angel slaying had been able to alleviate.

Speaking of Angels… Uriel. Seeing that fucker again for the first time since Tabitha died had been an experience I was unprepared for, despite the number of dreams and fantasies I'd had about it. Knowing he'd escaped again pissed me the fuck off.

But he'd get his, I guarantee it.

"Alright, brother. You can come in, but make it quick," Cole finally answered. I turned just as the door to his realm opened and I wasted no time in entering.

I spotted Mika almost immediately, and I couldn't help the relieved smile that broke out at the sight of her alive and well. She smiled at me and hurried to throw her arms around me.

"You're alive," I murmured as I hugged her tightly, closing my eyes on the reality of the moment. A small pang twisted my gut when I couldn't help wishing Tabitha had come back too.

"And so are you," she replied with a choked laugh.

"Thanks to you," I pointed out, letting her go when I felt Cole's ire rise. It was fun to piss him off, but I was more concerned about looking Mika over again. Guilt washed over me for the hundredth time when I replayed the fight at the warehouse. She'd been stabbed while saving me. Her concentration had been elsewhere, she'd poured so much of her energy into me that there had barely been any left for her. If I hadn't gotten myself stabbed, Mika never would have died in the first place and we could have saved ourselves this whole ordeal.

Mika shook her head, her expressive green eyes shining with understanding. "I was doing what I do best. Don't you dare feel guilty about it," she scolded and hugged me again.

"Okay, that's enough. One hug was plenty," Cole cut in possessively. I met my brother's angry gaze over his mate's shoulder and smiled before pulling away.

"You look better, brother," I pointed out. Seeing him as distraught as he was, was not a sight I wished to experience again. I could, however, understand his grief. I couldn't imagine I'd looked much better when I lost Tabitha.

Cole squirmed uncomfortably at the memory of how he'd been and that we'd all been there to bear witness to his depression. I decided to let the subject drop when he simply nodded but said nothing else.

"What happened to Uriel?" Mika asked after a moment, and my jaw automatically clenched at hearing that asshole's name.

"He got away," I ground out.

"For now," Cole added. My gaze snapped to his, and the look on his face told me he'd be right there with me whenever I wanted to go hunting again. I nodded once to indicate I understood before I drew in a cleansing breath and clutched my book with both hands.

"I actually have another reason for visiting other than to see you both," I announced, indicating toward the couches so we could sit.

We spent the next few minutes going over what I'd learned about the prophecy, what it meant for all of us, and also the news that we could have children with our mates. The look on Cole and Mika's face was priceless but I wanted to get past all this stuff so I could get to what I really wanted to know.

Tomika was hiding something, and I knew what it was, but I needed her to trust me with the information. I needed her to let me in so I could do what I'd promised Tabitha I would do all those centuries ago.

"Mika... just tell me already," Cole said quickly.

She looked at her mate with wide eyes and he raised an eyebrow at her. "Nova and I have known since your first day here that you've been holding something back. Surely you know you can trust us by now."

Mika bit down on her lower lip as she considered what he'd said, and I held my breath as I waited impatiently to see if she'd finally cave, if she'd tell me what I already knew but trust me with it anyway.

Slowly, her gaze rose to meet mine and I felt my heart skip a beat.

"I think you already know," she whispered.

I nodded slowly, not wanting to scare her off telling us now, when all I wanted to do was scream it from the rooftops.

"Know what?" Cole demanded, frustrated.

"You're a twin," I announced, excitement burning deep within me.

Cole's eyes widened as his head turned sharply to look at his mate once more. "Really?"

Mika nodded and sighed, and then jumped into explaining her story. She and her twin were separated at seven years old when they were put into the foster system. She hasn't seen or spoken to her since, but she wanted to keep her existence a secret after learning how Demons and Angels were hunting Witches. If her sister had been able to remain hidden as well, then she was free, and Mika didn't want her freedom taken from her sister as it had been with her.

"While I don't want her held anywhere against her will, I don't want her caught by the Angels either," Mika told me, her eyes on me, her gaze purposeful, pointed.

My heart began to beat in overdrive and I forced myself to stay still when all I wanted was to leap to my feet and get searching immediately.

"Only you, Nova. I only trust *you* to find her," Mika whispered.

I leaned forward, making sure she could see the honesty on my face when I spoke next. "I promised your ancestor, Tabitha, that she and her family would be safe." Guilt jabbed at me for fucking up so completely, but I pushed it aside for now. "I failed when she was alive. And when you came back, I thought that was my second chance to redeem myself. Your family almost always produces female twins. I thought you had to have a sister out there, unless something happened to her."

"Will you find her? Keep her safe?" Mika asked, vulnerability and hope shining in her eyes.

"You have my word, Mika. I will find her and protect her with my life."

Mika glared. "She will not be a prisoner."

I grinned and shook my head. "If she is anything like you, like your ancestors, that would be impossible."

When Mika sighed next, it was as if a weight had been lifted from her shoulders. "Thank you, Nova. I know she'll be safe with you."

I nodded and took several seconds to absorb the confirmation I'd been waiting for before I turned to my brother.

"I will head out to look for her in the next couple of days. In the meantime... We found Krae. He's in my realm."

Cole's eyes flashed dangerously. "You found the traitorous bastard?"

I got to my feet. "I thought you might like to be a part of the interrogation."

I waited as Cole looked to Mika, a silent conversation passing between them before he turned back to me with a grin that could only be classed as *evil*.

"Let's go pay him a visit."

~

Hours later I made my way back to my realm and fell backward onto the cushioned lounge chair in front of the fire.

Krae was a sobbing mess, and I found it disgusting that he'd broken so easily. No, we hadn't been easy on him, but I held my Knights to a high standard, and I'd expected him to hold out longer than he had. Oh well, I'd give him tonight to recover, but his torture was *far* from over.

Shaking my head, I closed my eyes, and as always, Tabitha's beautiful face was there on the back of my eyelids.

Her bloodline survived. Someone got out.

I frowned and blinked a few times. It just seemed so impossible. I remembered everyone being herded into the house, and I remembered their screams when the house went up in flames. I looked for Wardwell decedents for decades and found no trace of any of them.

So how had it continued?

Something in my head felt… rusty. Like a screw was coming loose, and there was something I needed to see. But I was worried about pulling at that loose sheet of metal, something telling me it was better off boarded up. At least for now.

Pushing to my feet, I wandered over to the bookcase on the other side of the room and pulled down that book with prophecies in it. I flicked to the relevant page and frowned.

"The sixth will save she he must be finding."

I read the words aloud for the umpteenth time, a tingle starting somewhere in the back of my mind.

Somehow, deep down, I knew I was on the search for my mate, and that I would finally be able to keep my promise to Tabitha, the one I'd told *no one* about.

The memory washed over me once more and I closed my eyes, seeing it all as if for the first time.

"Will you come find me?" she'd whispered.

"Nothing short of death will stop me from finding you again, moya lyubov'. I will look for you in this life and the next, and all the ones that follow."

Determination filled me as I slammed the book shut.

I am coming, my love. And when I finally find you, I will never let you go.

$\sim$ END $\sim$

THANK YOU FOR READING

BEFORE THE FIRST

A KINGS OF HELL PREQUEL

DID YOU KNOW…
I HAVE TWO OTHER PEN NAMES?

I know that seems like overkill, but there is a method to my madness.

Books under the name **Alexis Maree** are for paranormal romances. Not everyone likes to read this genre, so I like to keep them separate.

Likewise, not everyone likes contemporary romances, so I have another pen name for those…**T. Maree.**

Then last, but certainly not least, are my sinfully sexy romances, the ones that border on the line of *"should she really put that down in print?"*
Some people don't like those kinds of spicy scenes, and so I decided to keep those separate from the rest under the name **Luna Maree.**

So, if you'd like to check out what else I've written, go onto my website.

Happy reading!

Alexis | Luna | T.